NAGUI[B MAHFOUZ]

RHADOPIS *of* NUBIA

Naguib Mahfouz is the most prominent author of Arabic fiction today. He was born in 1911 in Cairo and began writing at the age of seventeen. His first novel was published in 1939. Since then he has written nearly forty novel-length works and hundreds of short stories. In 1988 Mr. Mahfouz was awarded the Nobel Prize in Literature. He lives in the Cairo suburb of Agouza with his wife and two daughters.

Anthony Calderbank is the translator of *Zaat* by Sonallah Ibrahim and two novels by Miral al-Tahawy, *The Tent* and *Blue Aubergine*.

THE FOLLOWING TITLES BY NAGUIB MAHFOUZ
ARE ALSO PUBLISHED BY ANCHOR BOOKS:

*The Beggar**
*The Thief and the Dogs**
*Autumn Quail**
The Beginning and the End
Wedding Song†
Respected Sir†
The Time and the Place and Other Stories
The Search†
Midaq Alley
The Journey of Ibn Fattouma
Miramar
Adrift on the Nile
The Harafish
Arabian Nights and Days
Children of the Alley
Echoes of an Autobiography
The Day the Leader Was Killed
Akhenaten, Dweller in Truth
Voices from the Other World

The Cairo Trilogy:
Palace Walk
Palace of Desire
Sugar Street

*†published as omnibus editions

RHADOPIS *of* NUBIA

A Novel of Ancient Egypt

RHADOPIS *of* NUBIA

A Novel of Ancient Egypt

NAGUIB MAHFOUZ

Translated from the Arabic
by Anthony Calderbank

ANCHOR BOOKS
A DIVISION OF RANDOM HOUSE, INC.
NEW YORK

FIRST ANCHOR BOOKS EDITION, MARCH 2005

 Published in the United States by Anchor Books, a division of Random House, Inc., New York, and simultaneously in Canada by Random House of Canada Limited, Toronto. Originally published in Arabic in 1943 as *Radubis*, and subsequently in English in hardcover in the United States by The American University in Cairo Press, Cairo and New York, in 2003.

Map courtesy of OasisPhoto.com

Cataloging-in-Publication Data is on file at the Library of Congress.

Anchor ISBN: 1-4000-7668-4

Book design by Oksana Kushnir

www.anchorbooks.com

Printed in the United States of America
10 9 8 7 6 5 4 3 2 1

Translator's Introduction

Egypt has a long history of popular uprising. The causes of the country's insurrections may have swung between oppressive rule, dispossession of the peasantry, starvation, and the foreign yoke, but one essential ingredient links them all: there are limits to what the people will tolerate. Not only does Merenra II, winner of Rhadopis's heart, ignore this to his peril, modern rulers too have seen that anger spill over, as Sadat did with the bread riots of 1977. It is the timely repetition of such displays of public anger that makes this account of the love of Pharaoh and the courtesan, and their violent and premature demise, so relevant today.

For Mahfouz, writing in the late 1930s, the most recent example of the people's yearning for justice, freedom, and an end to tyranny was the 1919 Revolution, which had taken place less than twenty years before. As a cry against foreign involvement in Egypt's affairs and the monarchy's obvious connivance with 'the outsider,' the British, at the expense of the people, the revolution had a long-lasting effect. Nationalism was in the air as Mahfouz penned his ancient Egyptian novels, with war brewing in Europe and fledgling superpowers about to battle it out across the globe.

Mahfouz had read widely on Egyptology and was familiar with many aspects of ancient Egyptian life and culture.

He saw common threads between the events of ancient days and his own contemporary world. The relationship between the ruler and the ruled, Pharaoh and his people, and the political instability and unrest that is born of weak and self-indulgent leadership were clearly as much a feature of Egyptian life then as they were in Mahfouz's day. Similarly, the characters who inhabit his pharaonic works, and the political intrigues and romantic episodes that propel their lives, would have seemed quite familiar in the royal diwans, government ministries, and fashionable salons of pre-revolutionary Egypt. It is in his knowledge of ancient Egypt, therefore, that Mahfouz was able to veil his thoughts on modern Egypt. As we read of the downfall of Merenra, who, obsessive and prideful, offends the sensibilities of his people, we are left to ponder if Mahfouz had something to say about the monarchy of his own day.

As well as illustrating Mahfouz's fondness for political allegory, the story of Rhadopis also shows his willingness to incorporate fate as an active role player in the development of his narrative. This is what gives the historical romance of Rhadopis its tragic edge. Objects falling as omens from the talons of majestic birds are a common feature of ancient tales, but the falcon choosing to drop his precious cargo in Pharaoh's lap indicates to the two lovers from the onset that players other than the physical human beings who surround them have a role in their destinies. Artists, politicians, lovers, and cynics in this novel debate the nature of coincidence, and the fates and other unseen forces, magical and divine, are never far away as Rhadopis and her young royal lover are driven inevitably toward their untimely and unhappy ends.

Mahfouz sacrifices historical accuracy, bringing disparate places and people together. The Rhadopis described by

Herodotus was supposedly a celebrated Thracian courtesan, while Mahfouz presents her as sprung from the masses of rural Egypt and fallen into immoral living (a common motif throughout much of his work). Although there was no Merenra II, the historical Merenra really was a troubled pharaoh who died after a brief reign in the Sixth Dynasty, but he would not have met Rhadopis in real history. It is Mahfouz who has brought them together. But collaging history in this way is no different than what the collective folk version of the past does too, and even though these pharaonic novels distort the factual events, there is no doubt that they paint a richly textured picture of the vicissitudes of court life in the Nile Valley thousands of years ago.

The language Mahfouz uses in *Rhadopis of Nubia* sounds distant and regal, echoing the strangeness of the sacerdotal incantations and pharaonic pronouncements, suiting the historic and solemn nature of the happenings; the feel is classical, even archaic. At the same time, the dialogue is lively and reminiscent of the colloquial, though no colloquial words are used, so the characters, even those who hail from among the common people, sound vibrant and realistic. Thus the English is archaic too and, I hope, both otherworldly and familiar.

Whereas the canons of Arabic textuality allow Mahfouz to repeat the same words many times, a variation in the vocabulary is preferred in the English. When Mahfouz repeats the Arabic words for fear, pain, sadness, and unease two, three, or four times hot upon the heels of one another to build dramatic atmosphere and regulate the rhythm, the translator into English needs to resort to its vast repertoire of synonyms, balancing the registers of Saxon and Latin roots, and making choices that can often lead to compromise. Working on a text by a master craftsman like Mahfouz, one is made only too painfully aware of the limitations of one's own literary abilities.

It is good to know that although languages are different, the same tales are told in all of them. Love transforms Rhadopis's life from a dull and tedious pretense into a joyous and radiant state of contentment for a while, and then she drinks from the bitter cup of disappointment, failure, and loss. It is a timeless and universal story Mahfouz relates here, and I am grateful to have had the opportunity to participate in bringing it to the reach of English-speaking readers. I would like to thank the American University in Cairo Press for entrusting me with this task, and my friends Abu Bakr Faizallah and Abdullah Bushra for their valuable suggestions.

RHADOPIS *of* NUBIA

A Novel of Ancient Egypt

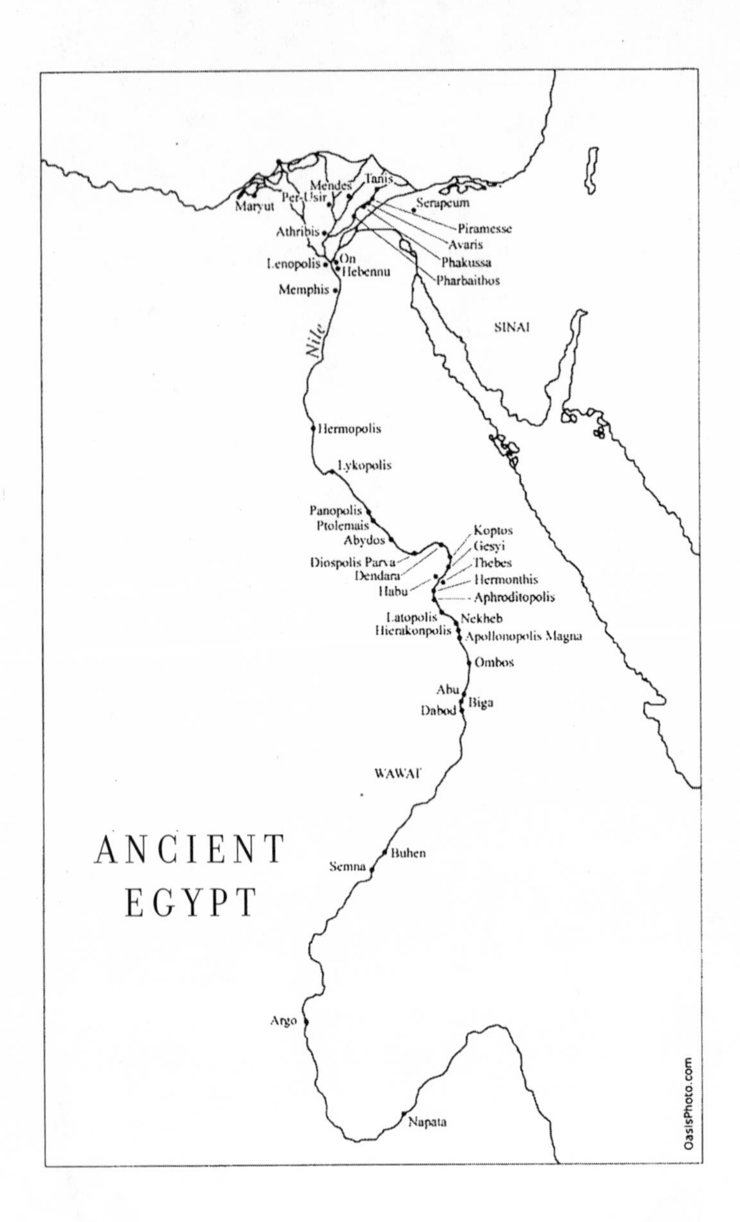
Maryut
Per-Usir
Mendes
Tanis
Serapeum
Athribis
Piramesse
Avaris
Phakussa
Pharbaithos
Lenopolis
On
Hebennu
Memphis
Nile
SINAI
Hermopolis
Lykopolis
Panopolis
Ptolemais
Abydos
Diospolis Parva
Dendara
Habu
Koptos
Gesyi
Thebes
Hermonthis
Aphroditopolis
Latopolis
Hierakonpolis
Nekheb
Apollonopolis Magna
Ombos
Abu
Dabod
Biga
WAWAT
ANCIENT
EGYPT
Buhen
Semna
Argo
Napata
OasisPhoto.com

The Festival of the Nile

The first light of dawn peered over the eastern horizon that morning in the month of Bashans, more than four thousand years ago. The high priest of the temple of the god Sothis gazed at the vast expanse of sky with tired eyes, for he had not slept the whole night.

Finding the object of his surveillance, his eyes lit upon Sirius, the auspicious star, its light twinkling in the heart of the firmament. His face glowed with jubilation and his heart quivered with joy. He prostrated himself on the hallowed floor of the temple and gave thanks, crying out at the top of his voice that the image of the god Sothis had appeared in the heavens, announcing to the inhabitants of the valley the glad tidings of the sacred River Nile's inundation. It was a message from His merciful and compassionate hands. The beautiful voice of the high priest woke the sleeping populace and they rose joyfully from their beds. They turned their faces to the sky until their eyes fixed upon the sacred star, and they repeated the incantation of the priest, their hearts awash with gratitude and delight. They left their houses and hurried to the bank of the Nile to witness the first ripples, bearers of bounty and good fortune. The voice of the priest of Sothis resounded through Egypt's still air, announcing the good news to the South: "Come celebrate the holy festival of the Nile!" And they tied up their belongings and set off, great and humble alike, from Thebes and Memphis, Harmunet and Sout and Khamunu, all heading for the capital Abu, in chariots speeding down the valley and boats plowing the billows.

Abu was the capital of Egypt. Its lofty structures were set upon huge slabs of granite, and the sand dunes in between them, long since tamed by the wondrous silt of the Nile, were awash with greenness and fertility. Acacia and doum trees grew there, as well as date palms and mulberries, and the fields were planted with herbs and vegetables and clover. There were vines in abundance and pastures and gardens watered by bubbling streams where flocks grazed. Pigeons and doves circled in the sky. The scent of flowers drifted on the fresh breeze and the chirping of nightingales mingled harmoniously with the songs of myriad birds.

In only a few days, Abu and its two islands, Biga and Bilaq, were packed with visitors. Houses filled up with guests and tents crowded the public squares. Throngs of people moved through the streets and gathered around the conjurers, singers, and dancers. A multitude of traders hawked their wares in the markets and the fronts of houses were decorated with banners and olive branches. The people's eyes were dazzled by the groups of royal guards from the island of Bilaq with their ornate uniforms and long swords. Bands of pious believers hastened to the temples of Sothis and the Nile, making vows and giving offerings. The songs of the minstrels mixed with the drunken cries of the revelers as a mood of unbridled joy and raucous entertainment pervaded the normally composed atmosphere of Abu.

Finally the day of the festival arrived. Everyone made their way to one place, the long road stretching between Pharaoh's palace and the hill upon which stood the temple of the Nile. The air was hot from the excitement in their breath and the earth strained under their weight. Many despaired of ever finding a place on land and went down to the boats and set sail to the temple hill, singing Nile songs to the accompaniment of flutes and lyres, and dancing to the beat of drums.

Soldiers lined the edges of the great road lances at the ready. At equal distances apart, life-size statues of the kings of the Sixth Dynasty had been erected, Pharaoh's father and forefathers. Those nearest to the front could see the pharaohs: Userkara, Teti I, Pepi I, Mohtemsawef I, and Pepi II.

The clamor of voices filled the air, each one impossible to distinguish, like the waves on a raging ocean, leaving no trace except an awesome, all-encompassing uproar. Now and then, however, an especially powerful voice would stand out, crying: "Glory be to Sothis who has brought us glad tidings!" or "Glory be to the sacred Nile god who brings life and fertility to our land!" And here and there voices requested the wines of Maryut and the meads of Abu, calling for merriment and forgetfulness.

One group of spectators stood together, chatting earnestly among themselves, indications of affluence and nobility showing upon their faces. One of them raised his eyebrows in wonder and contemplation, and said, "How many pharaohs have looked down upon this multitude and beheld this great day? Then they all passed away as if they had never existed, and yet in their day, how those pharaohs filled the eyes and hearts of their people."

"Yes," said another. "They have gone, just as we all will go, and there they will rule a world more glorious than this one. Look at the position I hold. How many will hold it in future generations, and relive the hopes and joys that flutter in our breasts at this moment? I wonder if they will talk about us as we are talking about them?"

"Surely there must be more to us than a simple mention by future generations? If only there was no death."

"Could this valley ever be wide enough to accommodate all those generations that have passed away? Death is as natural as life. What is the value of eternity as long as we eat our fill after going hungry, grow old after being young, and know despair after joy?"

"How do you think they live in the world of Osiris?"

"Wait, and you will know soon enough."

Another one said, "This is the first time the gods have granted me the pleasure of seeing Pharaoh."

"I have seen him before," his friend remarked, "on the day of the great coronation, some months ago in this very spot."

"Look at the statues of his mighty ancestors."

"You'll see that he greatly resembles his grandfather Mohtemsawef I."

"How handsome he is!"

"Indeed, indeed. Pharaoh is a beautiful young man. There is none like him in his imposing height and his unmistakable comeliness."

"I wonder what legacy he will bequeath?" asked one of the group. "Will it be obelisks and temples, or memories of conquest in the north and south?"

"If my intuition serves me right I suspect it will be the latter."

"Why?"

"He is a most courageous young man."

The other shook his head cautiously: "It is said that his youth is headstrong, and that His Majesty is possessed of violent whims, is fond of romance, enjoys extravagance and luxury, and is as rash and impetuous as a raging storm."

The one listening laughed quietly and whispered, "And what is so surprising about that? Are not most Egyptians fond of romance and enjoy extravagance and luxury? Why should Pharaoh be any different?"

"Lower your voice, man. You know nothing about the matter. Did you not know that he clashed with the men of the priesthood from the first day he ascended to the throne? He wants money to spend on constructing palaces and planting gardens while the priests are demanding the allotted share of the gods and the temples in full. The young king's predecessors bestowed influence and wealth upon the priesthood, but he eyes it all greedily."

"It is truly regrettable that the king should begin his reign in confrontation."

"Indeed. And do not forget that Khnumhotep, the prime minister and high priest, is a man of iron will and most intractable. And then there is the high priest of Memphis, that illustrious city whose shining star has begun to wane under the rule of this glorious dynasty."

The man was alarmed at the news, which had not found his ears before, and he said, "Then let us pray that the gods will grant men wisdom, patience, and forethought."

"Amen, amen," said the others with heartfelt sincerity.

One of the spectators turned toward the Nile and prodded his companion in the elbow, saying, "Look at the river, my friend. Whose beautiful boat is that coming from the island of Biga? It is like the sun rising over the eastern horizon."

His friend craned his neck to see the river and saw a wonderful barge, not one of the large ones, but neither too small, green in color like a verdant island floating on the water. From a distance, its cabin seemed high, though it was not possible to make out who was inside. At the top of its mast was a huge billowing sail and the oars on either side moved in solemn harmony, pulled by hundreds of arms.

The man wondered for a moment, then said, "Perhaps it belongs to one of the wealthy men of Biga."

A man standing nearby was listening to their conversation, and looking at them, shook his head. "I would wager that you two gentlemen are guests here," he said.

The two men laughed and one of them said, "You would be right to do so, my dear sir. We are from Thebes. Two of the many thousands who have answered the call of the illustrious festival and hastened to the capital from all nations. Could that majestic barge belong to one of your notable citizens?"

The man smiled mysteriously and shook his finger at them in warning as he said, "Be in good spirits, my dear gentlemen. The boat does not belong to a man but rather to a woman. Indeed, it is the ship of a beautiful courtesan whom the people of Abu and its two islands Biga and Bilaq know well."

"And who, pray, is this beautiful woman?"

"Rhadopis, Rhadopis the enchantress and seductress, queen of all hearts and passions."

The man pointed to the island of Biga and continued: "She lives over there in her enchanting white palace. That is where her lovers and admirers head to compete for her affections and to stimulate the flow of her compassion. You may be lucky enough to see her, may the gods protect your hearts from harm."

The eyes of the two men, and many others in the crowd, turned once again toward the boat, their faces filled with curiosity, as the barge slowly neared the shore and the skiffs and fishing boats scrambled to make way for it. As the barge inched forward, it gradually disappeared behind the hill on which the temple of the Nile stood, the bow passing first out of sight, then the cabin. When at last it came to rest at the wharf, all that could be seen of it was the top of the mast and part of the billowing sail that surged in the breeze like a banner of love that offers shade to hearts and souls.

A brief moment passed and then four Nubians, coming from the shore, strode into view and proceeded to open a way through the heaving throng of people. Following close behind came four others carrying on their shoulders a sumptuous palanquin, the like of which only princes and nobles possess. In it was a young woman of ravishing beauty, reclining on pillows, her tender-skinned arm leaning upon a cushion. In her right hand she held a fan of ostrich feathers, and in her eyes, gazing proudly at the distant horizon, a sleepy, dreamlike look shimmered, fit to pierce all creatures to the quick.

The small procession edged slowly forward, eyes transfixed upon it from all quarters, until at length it reached the front row of spectators. There the woman leaned forward a little with a neck like a gazelle, and from her rosy lips sprang such words the like of which the soul desires. The slaves drew to a halt and stood motionless in their places like bronze statues. The woman resumed her former posture and was lost once again in her dreams as she waited for Pharaoh's procession which, without a doubt, she had come to see.

Only her top half could be seen. Those fortunate enough to be near her caught glimpses of her jet-black hair adorned with threads of shining silk as it fell about the radiant orb of her face and cascaded onto her shoulders in a halo of night, as though it were a divine crown. Her cheeks were like fresh roses and her delicate mouth was parted slightly to reveal teeth like jasmine petals in the sunlight set in a ring of cloves. Her dark, deep, heavy-lidded eyes had a glint in them that knew love as the creation knows its creator. Never before had a face been seen in which such beauty had chosen to take up lasting abode.

The sight of her had everyone enthralled and stirred the waning hearts of tired old men. Fiery looks rained down on her from all directions, so hot they would have melted slate had they encountered it on their way. Sparks of loathing flew from the women's eyes, and in whispers the discussion went from mouth to mouth among those standing around her: "What an enchanting and seductive woman she is."

"Rhadopis. They call her the mistress of the island."

"Her beauty is overpowering. No heart can resist it."

"It brings only despair to him who beholds it."

"You are right. No sooner had I set eyes upon her than an untameable stirring arose in my breast. I was weighed down by the burdens of an oppressive tyranny, and feeling a devilish rebellion, my heart turned and shunned what was before me, and I was overcome by disappointment and unending shame."

"That is most regrettable. For I see her as a paragon of joy well worthy of worship."

"She is a calamitous evil."

"We are too weak to handle such ravishing beauty."

"Lord have mercy on her lovers!"

"Do you not know that her lovers are the cream of the men of the kingdom?"

"Truly?"

"To love her is an obligation upon the notables of the upper classes, as though it were a patriotic duty."

"Her white palace was built by the brilliant architect Heni."

"And Ani, governor of the island of Biga, furnished it with works of art from Memphis and Thebes."

"How wonderful!"

"And Henfer, the master sculptor, carved its statues and adorned its walls."

"Indeed he did, and General Tahu, commander of Pharaoh's guard, gave some of his priceless pieces."

"If all of them are competing for her affections, then who is the lucky man she will choose for herself?"

"Do you think you'll find a lucky man in this unfortunate city?"

"I do not think that woman will ever fall in love."

"How do you know? Maybe she will fall in love with a slave or an animal."

"Never. The strength of her beauty is colossal, and what need does strength have of love?"

"Look at the hard, narrow eyes. She has not tasted love yet."

A woman who was listening to the conversation became annoyed. "She's nothing but a dancer," she said, her voice full of spite. "She was brought up in a pit of depravity and corruption. Since she was a child she has given herself over to wantonness and seduction. She has learned to use her makeup skillfully and now takes on this enticing and deceptive form."

Her words were too much for one of the infatuated men.

"Do not speak thus in front of the gods, woman," he berated her. "Do you not know yet that her wondrous beauty is not the only wealth the gods have endowed her with? For Thoth has not been mean with wisdom and knowledge."

"Nonsense. What does she know about wisdom and knowledge when she spends all her time seducing men?"

"Every evening her palace receives a select group of politicians, wise men, and artists. It is no wonder then, as is widely known of her, that she understands wisdom more than most, is well versed in politics, and most discerning in matters of art."

"How old is she?" someone asked.

"They say she is thirty."

"She cannot be a day over twenty-five."

"Let her be as old as she wishes. Her comeliness is ripe and irresistible, and seems destined never to fade."

"Where did she grow up?" inquired the asker again. "And where is she from?"

"Only the gods know that. For me it is as if she has always been there in her white palace on the island of Biga."

All of a sudden a peculiar-looking woman cut through the assembled ranks. Her back was bent like a bow and she leaned on a thick stick. Her white hair was matted and disheveled, her fangs long and yellow, and her nose crooked. Her stern eyes emitted a fearsome light from beneath two graying eyebrows and she wore a long, flowing gown girded at the waist with a flaxen cord.

"It is Daam," cried those who saw her, "Daam, the sorceress!" She paid no heed to them as her bony feet carried her on her way. She claimed to be able to see the invisible world and to know the future. She would offer her supernatural power in exchange for a piece of silver, and those who gathered round her were either afraid of her or mocked her. On her way, the sorceress met a young man and offered to tell his fortune. The youth agreed, for if truth be told, he was drunk and staggering and his legs could hardly carry him. He pressed a piece of silver into her palm as he gazed at her with half-sleepy eyes.

"How old are you, lad?" she asked him in her hoarse voice.

"Twelve cups," he answered, unaware of what he was saying.

The crowd roared with laughter, but the woman was furious and threw away the piece of silver he had given her and went on her way, which never seemed to end. Suddenly another young man blocked her way, sneering: "What happenings await me, woman?" he asked her rudely.

She looked at him a moment, angry and embittered, then said, "Rejoice! Your wife will betray you for the third time."

The people laughed and applauded her as the young man retreated in embarrassment, the arrow having been deflected to return and pierce his own breast. The sorceress walked on until she reached the courtesan's palanquin and, keen to test her generosity, she stopped before it, smiling slyly as she called to the woman sitting inside: "Shall I read your stars, O lady who is so carefully guarded?"

The courtesan did not appear to have heard the voice of the sorceress.

"My lady!" the old woman shouted. Rhadopis looked toward her, seemingly in panic, then turned her head quickly away, for anger had touched her.

"Believe me," the old woman told her, "there is none in all this clamoring crowd who has need of me today like you do," whereupon one of the slaves approached the old woman and stood between her and the palanquin. The incident, despite its insignificance, would have aroused the interest of those standing nearby had not the shrill sound of a horn cut through the air. Immediately the soldiers lining the road raised their horns to their lips and blew a long continuous note, and all the people knew that Pharaoh's entourage had set off, and that soon Pharaoh would leave the palace on his way toward the temple of the Nile. Everyone forgot what they had been doing and gazed toward the road, necks craned, senses fine-tuned.

Long minutes passed, then the vanguard of the army appeared marching in ranks to the strains of martial music. At their head was the garrison of Bilaq with their assorted war gear, marching behind their standard, which bore the image of a hawk. The soldiers were met with a wave of tumultuous applause.

Then a hush fell over the crowd as a troop of infantry bearing lances and shields drew into view, their music infused with the spirit of the god Horus and their standard adorned with his image. Their lances were pointed straight up at the sky with geometrical precision, forming parallel lines in the air the length and breadth of the ranks.

Next came the great battalion of archers with their bows and quivers of arrows marching behind their standard, which bore a royal staff. They took a long time to pass.

Then in the distance, with a clattering and a jangling and a neighing of horses, the chariots appeared, moving in rows of ten, arranged so precisely they looked as if a pen had drawn them. Each chariot was drawn by two magnificent chargers and carried a charioteer with his sword and javelin, and an armored archer holding his bow in one hand and his quiver in the other. When they saw them, the spectators remembered the conquests of Nubia and Mount Sinai. They saw the troops in their mind's eye, swarming over the plains and down the valleys like vultures swooping from the sky, the enemy scattering before them in terror as destruction fell upon them. The crowd's excitement burned in their veins and their cries rent the heavens.

Then the solemn cortege of Pharaoh appeared, led by the royal chariot, followed immediately by crescent formations of chariots in fives bearing princes and ministers with the chief priests, the thirty judges of the regions, the commanders of the army, and the governors of the provinces. Finally, a detachment of the royal guard with Tahu at their head brought up the rear.

Pharaoh stood straight and tall in his chariot, solemn of mien like a granite statue that inclines neither right nor left, his eyes set firmly on the distant horizon, heedless of the great crowd and the cries ringing from the depths of their hearts.

The double crown of Egypt was set upon his head, while in one hand he gripped the royal flail and in the other the scepter. Over his regal garments he wore a leopard skin cape in celebration of the religious festival.

Hearts were filled with joy and excitement, and such was the din rising into the air that the birds in the sky flew away in fear. Rhadopis was carried away by the fervor and a sudden surge of life rushed through her, lighting up her face with a radiant light as she clapped her tender hands.

Then suddenly, above the noise of the crowd, one voice cried out in haste: "Long live His Excellency Khnumhotep!" Dozens of other voices echoed the call, which caused great unease and consternation, and the people looked round to see who could be so bold as to call out the prime minister's name in young Pharaoh's hearing and who had lent support to this audacious and unimaginable challenge.

The cry left no noticeable trace and had not the slightest effect on any in the king's entourage, thus the procession continued on its way until at last it reached the temple hill. The chariots pulled up all at once and two princes carrying a cushion of ostrich feathers adorned with a cover of gold lace walked up to Pharaoh's chariot. The king stepped on to it and blew into a horn. The soldiers saluted and the musicians of the royal guard played the anthem of the sacred Nile as Pharaoh solemnly ascended the steps leading up the hill. He was followed by the great and mighty of his kingdom: generals, ministers, and governors, and at the door of the great temple waited the priests, laid in prostration before him. As Lord Chamberlain Sofkhatep announced the arrival of Pharaoh, the high priest of the temple rose to his feet and bowed, and hiding his eyes with his hands, spoke in a low voice: "The servant of the god of the sacred Nile is honored to extend humble and sincere greetings to our lord, Master of Upper and Lower Egypt, Son of Ra, Lord of the Radiant Ones."

Pharaoh extended the scepter and the high priest kissed it reverently. The priests stood up and fell into two rows so that Pharaoh might pass. His retinue followed him into the Great Hall of the Altar, which was lined on all sides with towering columns. They circled the sanctuary as the priests burned incense; its smell wafted through the temple and its smoke hovered over the heads lowered in reverence and humility. Some of the chamberlains brought in a bull that had been sacrificed and placed it on the altar as an offering and oblation. Then Pharaoh recited the customary words: "I stand before you, O Sacred God, having purified myself and presented this sacrifice as an offering to you, that you may bestow your bounty on the land of this good valley and its faithful people."

The priests repeated the prayer in resonant, moving voices that overflowed with faith and piety as they raised their faces to the sky, their arms open wide. All present repeated the prayer, and as the sound of their voices carried outside the temple, the people began to recite it until before long, not a single tongue remained that had not uttered the prayer of the sacred Nile. Then the king walked on, accompanied by the high priest and followed by the men of the kingdom, into the Hall of Columns with its three parallel vaults. They stood in two rows, with the king and the servant of the god in the middle, reciting the anthem of the sacred Nile in trembling voices, their hearts astir in their breasts, as the sound of their voices echoed through the grave and solemn blackness of the temple.

The high priest ascended the steps leading to the Eternal Chamber. As he neared the door to the Holy of Holies, he took out the sacred key and opened the great door, then, turning to one side, prostrated himself in prayer. The king followed and entered the divine chamber where the statue of the Nile in its celestial barge resided, then closed the door behind him. The large chamber with its high ceiling was dark and imposing. Near the curtain, which was drawn over the statue of the god, candles were set on tables of shining gold. The solemn aura of the place penetrated deep into the great king's heart, and his senses grew dull. Reverently, he approached the holy curtain and pulled it aside with his hand. Then, bending his back, which was not wont to bend, he genuflected on his right knee and kissed the foot of the statue. He retained his dignity, but the signs of worldly glory and pride were gone from his face and its surface now wore the pale hue of piety and humility. Pharaoh prayed for a long time and, absorbed in his worship, he forgot his ancient glory and worldly might.

When he had finished he kissed the sacred foot once again, stood up, and drew shut the holy curtain. He withdrew to the door with his face toward the god until he breathed the air of the outer hall and then closed the door behind him.

The congregation greeted Pharaoh with prayers and walked behind him to the Great Hall of the Altar, then followed him out of the temple, up to the brim of the hill that looked out over the Nile. When the people thronging the decks of the boats saw Pharaoh and his court, they started to cheer and wave their standards and brandish their staffs in the air. The high priest stepped forward to read the traditional address and, unrolling the sheet of papyrus in his hands, he read out in a resounding voice: "Peace be upon you, O Nile, whose inundation fills the valley, proclaiming life and joy. For months you reside in the Netherworld, and when you hear the beseeching of your servants, your great heart is filled with compassion for them. You come out of the darkness into the light, to flow abundantly down the belly of the valley. The earth bursts forth with life and soon the plants are trembling with joy and the desert is consumed beneath a carpet of velvet. The gardens are in bloom and the fields are awash with green. The birds are singing and all hearts are cheered with ecstasy and joy, for the naked are clothed and the hungry are fed, the thirsty are given to drink, and maidens and young men are joined in matrimony. The land of Egypt is consumed in happiness and delight. Come, glory be to You, come, glory be to You."

The temple priests recited the anthem of the Nile to the strains of lyres, flutes, and pipes, and a sweet and mellow rhythm flowed from the drums.

As the music drifted on the wind, Prince Nay approached Pharaoh and handed him a roll of papyrus sealed with wax, containing the anthem of the sacred Nile. The king took it and raised it to his forehead. Then he let it fall into the Nile where the bouncing waves carried it noisily to the north.

Pharaoh proceeded back down the hill and stepped into his chariot and the procession returned as it had come, effusing greatness and glory, to be hailed by a million hearts of his loyal subjects, all sharing in the buzz of excitement and the intoxication of joy.

The Sandal

Pharaoh's procession returned to the royal seraglio, with the king managing to maintain his dignity and bearing until he was alone. Only then did the anger show on his handsome face and unnerve the slave girls who were removing his apparel. His jugular vein was swollen with blood and his muscles tense. He was furious beyond belief and extremely volatile. He would not rest until those responsible were severely punished. The insolent cry was still ringing in his ears. He thought it a brazen intrusion upon his desires and he cursed and raged and vowed to wreak havoc and destruction.

Custom dictated that he should wait a whole hour before he met the grandees of the kingdom, who had come from all over the country to attend the festival of the Nile, but he did not have the patience and he rushed like a swirling wind to the queen's chambers and flung open the door. Queen Nitocris was sitting with her handmaidens, a look of peace and contentment glowing in her clear eyes. When the maidens saw the king and beheld the anger blazing in his face they rose to their feet nervous and confused, bowed to him and the queen, and withdrew in great haste. The queen remained sitting for a moment, looking at him intently with her peaceful eyes. Then she rose gracefully to her feet, walked over to him and, standing on her tiptoes, kissed his shoulder, asking, "Are you angry also, my lord?"

He was in dire need of someone to talk to about the fire ignited in his blood, and was glad of her question.

"As you see, Nitocris," he declared.

The queen realized immediately, knowing his ways so well, that her first duty was to soothe his anger whenever it raged. She smiled and said softly, "It is more becoming of a king to behave reasonably."

He shrugged his broad shoulders dismissively, saying, "Are you asking me to behave reasonably, Queen?" he scoffed. "Reasonableness is a false and insincere garment in which the weak masquerade."

The queen was clearly pained. "My lord," she asked, "why are you uneasy about virtue?"

"Am I truly Pharaoh? And do I not enjoy youth and strength? How then should I desire and not obtain that which I desire? How can my eyes look at the lands of my kingdom, and a slave blocks my way and tells me, 'That will never belong to you'?"

She put her hand on his arm and tried to lead him into the diwan, but he moved away and began to pace up and down the room muttering angrily to himself.

In a voice that betrayed deep sorrow, the queen said, "Do not picture things in this way. Always remember that the priests are your faithful subjects and that the temple lands were granted over to them by our forefathers. Now those lands have become the inalienable right of the clergy and you want to take them back, my lord. It is no wonder they are uneasy."

"I want to build palaces and temples," said the young king. "I want to enjoy a high and happy life. The fact that half of the land in the kingdom is in the hands of the priesthood will not stand in my way. Is it right that I should be tormented by my desires like the poor? To hell with this empty wisdom. Do you know what happened today? As I was passing, one of the crowd called out the name of that man Khnumhotep. Don't you see, Queen? They are openly threatening Pharaoh."

The queen was astonished and her gentle face turned yellow as she mumbled a few words under her breath.

"What has come over you, My Queen?" said the king in a sardonic tone.

No doubt she felt irritation and dismay, and if it were not for the fact that the king was furious to the point of distraction she would not have tried to conceal her own anger, and so, controlling her turbulent feelings with a will of iron, she said calmly, "Leave this talk for later. You are about to meet the men of your kingdom with Khnumhotep at their head. You should receive them in the proper and official way."

Pharaoh looked at her mysteriously, then with ominous composure said, "I know what I want and what I should do."

At the appointed time, Pharaoh received the men of his kingdom in the Great Ceremonial Hall. He listened to the speeches of the clergy and the opinions of the governors. Many noticed that the king was not himself. As everyone was leaving, the king asked his prime minister to stay behind and talked with him in private for a good while. People were curious, but none dared to inquire. When the prime minister reappeared there were many who tried to read his face in the hope of discerning the slightest clue as to the subject of his audience, but his mien was as expressionless as rock.

The king ordered his two closest counselors, Sofkhatep the lord chamberlain and Tahu the commander of the guard, to go on ahead and wait for him at a spot by the lake in the royal gardens, the site of their evening conversations.

He walked along the shaded green paths with a look of relaxation on his swarthy face, as if he had quelled the violent anger that had so recently spurred him to vengeance. He walked unhurriedly, breathing in the fragrant aroma the trees sent out to greet him, and his eyes wandered over the flowers and fruits until at length he reached the gorgeous lake. He found his two men waiting for him—Sofkhatep, with his tall thin body and graying hair, and Tahu, strong and muscular, reared on the backs of horses and chariots.

Both men scrutinized the face of the king in an effort to fathom his inner thoughts and ascertain the policy he would advise them to follow in regard to the priests. They had heard the audacious cry, which had been considered by all and sundry a threat to Pharaoh's authority. They had expected it to provoke a severe reaction in the young king, and when they learned that he had asked his prime minister to stay behind after the meeting, they were both filled with apprehension. Sofkhatep was worried about the consequences of the king's anger, for he always advised caution and patience and believed that the problem of the temple lands should be dealt with equitably. Tahu, on the other hand, was hoping that the king's anger would lead him to side with his own opinion and order the seizure of the temple properties thus giving the priests a final warning.

The two loyal men looked into their lord's face in hope, yet enduring painful unease. But Pharaoh kept a tight rein on his emotions, and studied them with an expression like the Sphinx. He knew what discomfiting thoughts were racing through their minds, and, as though wishing to torment them a little longer, he sat down on his throne and did not say a word. He motioned them to be seated and the look of serious concern returned to his face.

"Today I have the right to feel anger and pain," he declared.

The two men understood what he meant, and the bold and insolent cry rang in their ears once again. Sofkhatep raised his hands out of distress and sympathy, and spoke in a trembling voice, "My lord, do not allow yourself to be caught up in pain and anger."

"It is not fitting that my lord should suffer pain," echoed Tahu firmly, "while in the kingdom no sword lies idly in its sheath, and there are men who would gladly sacrifice their lives for him. Truly those priests, despite their knowledge and experience, are deviating from the way of good sense. They are acting rashly, and laying themselves open to an onslaught the like of which they will have no power to avert."

The king lowered his head and looked at the ground beneath his feet. "I am wondering," he said, "if one of my fathers or forefathers would have been greeted with the cry that greeted me today. Why, I have only been on the throne a matter of months."

Tahu's eyes shone with a fleeting frightening light. "Force, my lord," he said with conviction. "Force. Your sacred forefathers were strong men. They exercised their will with a determination as mighty as the mountains and a sword as relentless as fate. Be like them my lord. Do not procrastinate, and do not engage them with reason and understanding. When you strike them, strike hard and show no quarter. Make the upstart forget who he is and extinguish the leanest hope in his heart."

Wise old Sofkhatep was unhappy with the words he heard. He mistrusted the zeal of him who had spoken them, and was fearful of the consequences.

"My lord," he said, "the priesthood is dispersed throughout the kingdom as blood through the body. Among its members are officials and judges, scribes and educators.

Their authority over the people is blessed by divine sanction from ancient times. We have no battle forces save the pharaonic guard and the guardians of Bilaq. A forceful strike might bring undesired consequences."

Tahu believed only in force. "Then what are we supposed to do, wise counselor?" he demanded. "Should we just sit back and wait for our enemy to fall upon us, and thus be rendered contemptible in his eyes?"

"The priests are not Pharaoh's enemies, may the gods forbid that Pharaoh should have any enemies among his people. The priesthood is a loyal and trustworthy institution. All that we can say against them is that their privileges are greater than need dictates. I swear that I have never despaired, not even for a single day, of finding an acceptable compromise that would fulfill my lord's desire and at the same time preserve the rights of the clergy."

The king was listening to them quietly, a mysterious smile etched upon his broad mouth, and when Sofkhatep finished speaking he gazed at them with mocking eyes and said quietly, "Do not trouble yourselves about the matter my dear faithful gentlemen. I have already shot my arrow."

The two men were taken aback. They looked at the king, hopeful yet apprehensive, Tahu being the one more inclined to hope, while Sofkhatep's face turned pale and he bit his lip as he waited in silence to hear the decisive word. At length the king spoke in a voice displaying arrogance and self-satisfaction: "I presume you already know that I kept the man behind after all the guests had left, and once the place was empty I started on him. I told him that the calling of his name in my hearing and under my very eyes was a despicable and treacherous thing to do, and I impressed upon him that I do not execute the noble and faithful of my people who cry out.

I could see he was uneasy and his face went white. He lowered his large head onto his narrow chest and opened his mouth to speak. Perhaps he wanted to apologize in his cold, quiet voice."

The king knitted his brow and was silent for a moment, then he continued, speaking in a more aggressive tone, "I interrupted him with a wave of my hand, and did not allow him to apologize. I explained to him firmly, reminding him that it was naïve and simple-minded to think that such a cry would detract me from the course I have set upon. I informed him that I had decided irrevocably to enjoin the property of the temples to the crown estates, and that from today onward nothing would be left to the temples save the lands and offerings they need."

The two men listened intently to the king's words. Sofkhatep's face was wan and drawn, revealing the bitterness of disappointment, while Tahu beamed with joy, as though he were listening to a pleasant ballad extolling his glory and greatness. The king continued, "Make no mistake, my decision surprised Khnumhotep, and disconcerted him. He appeared anxious and he beseeched me, saying, 'The temple lands belong to the gods. Their produce goes mostly to the common people and the poor, and is spent on learning and moral education.' He tried to go on but I stopped him with a gesture of my hand and said to him, 'It is my will. You are to enforce it without further delay.' Thereupon I told him the meeting was ended."

Tahu could hardly contain his joy: "May all the gods bless you, my lord."

The king smiled calmly, and shot a glance at Sofkhatep's face in its hour of defeat. The king felt sympathy toward him and said, "You are a loyal and faithful man, Sofkhatep, and a wise counselor. Do not be disappointed that your opinion has been disregarded."

"I am not one of those vain persons, my lord," he said, "who are swift to anger if their advice goes unheeded, not out of fear of the consequences, but to preserve their dignity. Even vanity can reach so far with such people that they hope an evil thing they warned about will happen so that those who doubted their ability may truly know it. I take refuge in the gods from the evil of vanity. It is only loyalty that dictates my advice, and the only thing that saddens me when it is ignored is the misgiving that my intuition might be true. All I ask from the gods is that they prove my forecast wrong so that my heart might be assured."

And as if to put the old man's mind at rest, Pharaoh said, "I have attained my desire. They will obtain nothing from me. Egypt worships Pharaoh and will be content with none but him."

The two men assented sincerely to their lord's words, but Sofkhatep was perturbed, and he struggled in vain to play down the danger of Pharaoh's decree, for he realized with a certain alarm that the priests would receive the momentous edict while they were gathered at Abu. There they would have ample opportunity to exchange opinions and disseminate their complaints, and they would return to their dioceses muttering their grievances. But although he had no doubt about the status of the priesthood and its influence on the hearts and minds of the common folk, he did not reveal his opinions, for he could see the king was happy, contented, and smiling, and he was unwilling to spoil the young man's mood. So he removed all expression from his face and drew a contented smile upon his lips.

"I have not felt such exhilaration," the king said delightedly, "since the day I defeated the tribes of Southern Nubia when my father was alive. Let us drink a toast to this happy victory."

The slave girls brought a jug of red Maryut and golden goblets. They filled the goblets to the brim and passed them round to the king and the two loyal men who drank heartily. The wine soon took its effect and Sofkhatep felt the troubling thoughts dissolve in his breast as his senses savored the fine vintage, and he shared with the king and the commander in their happiness. They sat silently, exchanging convivial looks of affection. The rays of the setting sun bathed in the shimmering water of the lake, which lapped against the bank close to their feet. The branches of the trees around them danced to the bird songs, and flowers sprang out amidst their leaves like sweet memories rising from deep within the mind. They surrendered to a drowsy wakefulness for not a little time until they were aroused by a strange event, which plucked them violently from their dreams—something fell from the sky into Pharaoh's lap. He leapt to his feet and the two men saw the object land at his feet. It was a golden sandal. They looked up in amazement and saw a magnificent falcon circling in the sky above the garden, its terrifying shrieks rending the air. The bird glared at them with blazing, censorious eyes, then, with a great flap of its mighty wings, it soared into the air and disappeared over the horizon.

They looked back at the sandal. The king picked it up and sat down to contemplate it with a look of surprise in his smiling eyes. The two men looked curiously at the sandal, exchanging looks of denial, astonishment, and consternation.

The king continued to inspect the sandal, then mumbled,

"It is a woman's sandal, no doubt about it. How beautiful and expensive it is."

"The falcon must have picked it up and carried it away," said Tahu as his eyes devoured the sandal.

The king smiled and said, "There is no tree in my garden that bears such fine fruit."

Sofkhatep spoke: "The general populace, my lord, believe that the falcon courts beautiful women, and that he ravishes the virgins he falls in love with and whisks them off to the mountaintops. Maybe that falcon was a lover who had been down to Memphis to buy sandals for his beloved, and his luck betrayed him and one dropped from his talons, and fell at my lord's feet."

The king looked at it again overjoyed, excited. "I wonder how he came by it?" he said. "I fear it may belong to one of the maidens who dwell in the sky."

"Or to one of the maidens who dwell on the earth," said Sofkhatep with interest, "who took it off with her clothes to bathe at the shore of some lake, and while she was naked in the water the falcon came and carried it away."

"And threw it into my lap. How amazing! It is as if he knows my love for beautiful women."

Sofkhatep smiled a meaningful smile. "May the gods make happy your days, my lord," he said.

Dreams shone in the king's eyes, and his entire face lit up. His brow softened and his cheeks flushed rosy red. He did not take his eyes off the sandal, as he asked himself who its owner might be, what she might look like, and if she were as beautiful as her footwear. She would have no idea that her sandal had fallen into the king's lap, and he wondered what it was that had let the Fates conspire to make him the sandal's destination. His eyes fell upon a picture engraved on the instep of the sandal and he pointed to it and said, "What a beautiful picture! It is a handsome warrior, holding his heart in his open hand to give it away."

His words struck a chord deep in the hearts of the two men and a fleeting light shone in their eyes as they looked at the sandal with renewed interest.

"Would my lord allow me to see the sandal for a moment?" said Sofkhatep.

Pharaoh gave it to him and the lord chamberlain looked at it, as did Tahu. Then Sofkhatep returned the sandal to the king and said, "My intuition was correct my lord. The sandal belongs to Rhadopis, the renowned courtesan of Biga."

"Rhadopis," exclaimed the king. "What a beautiful name. Who, I wonder, is she who is called it?"

A feeling of apprehension gripped Tahu's heart and his eyes twitched: "She is a dancer my lord. She is known by all the people of the South."

Pharaoh smiled. "Are we not of the South?" he said. "Truly the eyes of kings may pierce the veil of the farthest horizon and yet be blind to what goes on under their very noses."

Tahu's perturbation increased and his face turned pale as he said, "She is the woman, my lord, upon whose door the men of Abu, Biga, and Bilaq have all knocked."

Sofkhatep knew well the fears that gripped his friend's heart and with a sly and mysterious smile he said, "In any case she is a paragon of femininity, my lord. The gods have made her to bear witness to their miraculous abilities."

The king looked from one man to the other and smiled, "By Lord Sothis, you two are the finest informed of all the South."

"In her reception hall, my lord, thinkers, artists, and politicians gather," said Sofkhatep softly.

"Truly, beauty is a bewitching master who allows us a daily glimpse into the miraculous. Is she the most beautiful woman you have ever set eyes on?"

Without pausing for a moment's thought Sofkhatep answered, "She is beauty itself, Your Majesty. She is an irresistible temptation, a desire that cannot be controlled. The philosopher Hof, who is one of her closest friends, has remarked quite correctly that the most dangerous thing a man can do in his life is to set eyes upon the face of Rhadopis."

Tahu breathed a sigh of resignation, shot a quick glance at the lord chamberlain who understood his intention, and said, "Her beauty, Your Majesty, is of a cheap and devilish nature. She does not withhold it from any who ask."

The king laughed aloud and said, "How the description of her intrigues me!"

"May the skies of Egypt rain down happiness and beauty upon my lord," said Sofkhatep. His words took Pharaoh's mind back to the falcon, and the young king was overcome by an enchanting sensation compounded by the fine description he had heard, with its delicate dream-like texture of temptation. And as if talking to himself he wondered out loud, "Was that falcon right or wrong to chose us as its target?"

Tahu glanced furtively at his lord's face as the latter pored over the object in his hand. "It is nothing but a coincidence, my lord," said the general. "The only thing that saddens me is to see that sullied sandal between the sacred hands of Your Majesty."

Sofkhatep eyed his colleague with a sly self-satisfied look, then said calmly, "Coincidence? Why, the very word, my lord, is seriously overused. It is taken to imply blind stumbling into the unexpected, yet nevertheless is invariably employed to explain the happiest encounters and the most glorious catastrophes. Nothing is left in the hands of the gods except the rarest minimum of logical events. It cannot, however, be so, my lord, for every event in this world is, beyond a shadow of a doubt, contrived by the will of a god or gods, and it is not possible that the gods would create any event, however great or paltry, in vain or jest."

Tahu was furious, and scarcely managing to stem the flood of insane anger that threatened to scatter his composure in the presence of the king, he said to Sofkhatep in a tone displaying censure and rebuke, "Do you, mighty Sofkhatep, wish to occupy the mind of my lord at this most auspicious hour, with such nonsense?"

"Life is seriousness and jest," said Sofkhatep quietly, "just as the day contains light and darkness. It is a wise man who in times of seriousness does not remember those things that bring him pleasure, and does not spoil the purity of his pleasure with matters of gravity. Who knows, great general, perhaps the gods have known all along about His Majesty's love of beauty and have sent to him this sandal at the hands of this wondrous falcon."

The king looked into their faces and, in an effort to bring some levity to the proceedings, said, "Will the two of you never agree for once? Be it as you wish, but in Tahu the younger man, I would have thought to find one inciting me to love, and in Sofkhatep the elder, one discouraging me from it. In any case, I feel I must incline to Sofkhatep's views on love, as I incline to Tahu's views on politics."

As the king rose, the two men stood up. He looked at the vast garden as it bade farewell to the sun dipping over the western horizon.

"We have a hard night's work ahead of us," he said as he started to walk away. "Until tomorrow, and we shall see."

Pharaoh departed with the sandal in his hand and the two men bowed reverently.

They found themselves alone once again facing each other—Tahu with his tall stature, broad chest, and steel muscles; and Sofkhatep, fine and slender with his deep, clear eyes and his great, beautiful smile.

Each of them knew what was going through the other's mind. Sofkhatep smiled and Tahu's brow knit into a frown, for the general could not take his leave of the chamberlain without saying something to unburden his troubled mind: "You have betrayed me, Sofkhatep, friend, after you could not confront me face-to-face."

Sofkhatep raised his eyebrows in denial and said, "How far your words are from the truth, General. What do I know of love? Do you not know that I am a fading old man, and that my grandson Seneb is a student at the university in On?"

"How easy it is for you to weave words, my friend, but the truth scoffs at that wise old tongue of yours. Was not your young heart once enamored of Rhadopis? Did it not grieve you that she gave to me that affection you did not win?"

The old man raised his hands in protest at the general's words saying, "Your imagination is not any smaller than the muscles on your right forearm, and the truth is, that if my heart ever once inclined to that courtesan, it was in the way of the wise who do not know greed."

"Would it not have been more becoming of you if you had not beguiled His Majesty's mind with her beauty out of respect for me?"

Sofkhatep looked surprised, and he spoke with true regret and concern, "Is it true that you find the matter so serious or have you had enough of my jesting?"

"Neither one nor the other, sir, but it grieves me that we always differ."

The lord chamberlain smiled, and said with his characteristic stoicism, "We shall always be bound by one unbreakable tie: loyalty to he who sits upon the throne."

The Palace of Biga

Pharaoh's cortege drew out of sight. The statues of the kings of the Sixth Dynasty were removed and the people pushed forward from both sides of the road to converge like waves, their breaths mingling, as if they were the sea parted by Moses pouring down upon the heads of his enemies. Rhadopis ordered her slaves to return to the barge. The flush of excitement that had engulfed her heart when Pharaoh appeared remained like a flame, pumping hot blood all through her body. He was just as she had imagined, a fresh young man with proud eyes, lithe figure, and sinewy well-defined muscles.

She had seen him before, on the day of the grand coronation a few months previously. He was standing in his chariot as he had today, tall and exceedingly handsome as he gazed into the distant horizon. That day she had wished, as she had wished today, that his eye might fall upon her.

She wondered why. Was it because she longed for her beauty to win the honor and esteem it deserved, or was it because she wanted deep down inside to see him as a human being, after having beheld him in all the sacredness of the gods, as one deserving of her worship? How would one ever understand such a longing, and did it really matter? For whatever its true nature, she wished it honestly, and she wished it with sincerity and great desire.

The courtesan remained absorbed in her reverie for a while, blissfully unaware of her small entourage struggling to make its way through the heaving crowd, and paying not the slightest attention to the thousands who, greedily and with great savoring, almost swallowed her up. She was carried onto her barge and stepped off the palanquin and into the cabin, where she sat down upon her small throne as if in a trance, hearing but not listening, looking but not seeing. The boat slipped through the calm waters of the Nile until it berthed at the steps leading up into the garden of her white palace, the pearl of the island of Biga.

The palace could be seen at the far end of the lush garden, which stretched right down to the banks of the river. It was surrounded by sycamores, and tall palm trees swayed in the breeze above so that it looked like a white flower blossoming in a luxuriant bower. She walked down the gangplank and stepped on to the polished marble stairway that led up between two granite walls into the garden. On either side were high obelisks engraved with the fine poetry of Ramon Hotep. Finally she reached the velvet lawns of the garden.

She passed through a limestone gateway upon which her name was carved in the sacred language. Set in the middle was a life-size statue of herself, sculpted by Henfer. The time he had spent working on it had been the happiest days of his life. He had depicted her sitting upon her throne as she was wont to do when receiving her guests. He had brilliantly captured the extraordinary beauty of her face, the firmness of her breasts, and her delicate feet. She emerged on a path lined on either side with trees whose branches had met and intertwined to shade those strolling below from the sun with a ceiling of flowers and green leaves. The ground was covered with grass and herbs, and to the right and left, other paths of the same description led off, those on the right to the garden's south wall and those on the left to its north wall. The path she had taken led to a vineyard where grapes clambered over trellises set on marble columns. A wood of sycamore spread out to her right and a grove of palms to her left, wherein had been built here and there pens for monkeys and gazelles, while statues and obelisks stood all around the borders, which seemed to extend as far as the eye could see.

Finally her feet led her to a pool of clear water. Lotus plants grew around the edges, and geese and ducks glided across the surface, while birds sang in the trees and the sweet smell of perfume mingled in the air with the nightingale's song.

She walked halfway around the pool and stood before the summer room. A number of her slave girls were there to wait upon her, and they bowed reverently as she entered, then stood awaiting her orders. The courtesan lay her body down on a shaded couch to rest, but she could not sit still for long and she jumped to her feet, shouting to her slave girls, "The people's hot breaths annoyed me. And the heat, how it exhausted me. Take off my clothes. I want to feel the cool water of the pool against my body."

The first slave girl approached her mistress and gently removed the veil which was woven with golden threads from eternal Memphis. Then two others came up and took off her silk cape to reveal a translucent chemise that covered her body from just above the breasts to below the knees. Two more slave girls followed and with gentle hands removed the lucky blouse to dazzle the world with the body now set free, in whose creation all the gods had joined, and in which each had demonstrated his art and ability.

Another slave girl approached and took out the clips from her jet-black hair, which cascaded over her body, covering it from her neck to her wrists. She bent over to untie her golden sandals and placed them by the edge of the pool. Her body swayed as she strode slowly down the marble steps into the water, which covered first her feet, then her legs and thighs, until she was immersed entirely in the still water, which took in the body's sweet smell and gave it cool peace in return. Relaxing, she surrendered to the water and let it caress her as she splashed and played without a care in the world. She swam for a long time, sometimes on her back, then on her belly, or on one of her sides.

She would have remained there in sweet oblivion had not a sudden scream of terror from her slave girls rung in her ears. She stopped swimming and, turning toward them, was just in time to see a huge falcon swoop down by the edge of the pool. The bird flapped its wings and Rhadopis let out a shriek of terror. She dived under the water shaking with fear, and with enormous effort she held her breath until she felt her lungs would burst. When she could bear it no longer, she raised her head cautiously out of the water and looked around nervously. She saw no trace of the bird, but when she looked up at the sky she could just make out the falcon nearing the horizon. She swam quickly to the side of the pool and staggered up the steps in a state of shock. She put on one of her sandals but then could not find the other and she looked for it awhile before she asked, "Where is the other one?"

"The falcon took it," said the slave girls nervously.

A look of sadness crossed her face but she did not have the time to express her distress, for she hurried into the summer room with the slave girls all around her drying droplets of water that shone like pearls off the ivory skin of her succulent body.

As sunset approached, Rhadopis prepared to receive her guests. Their numbers grew greatly during the days of the festival, which drew people to the South from all over the land, and she dressed in her most beautiful clothes and put on her finest jewelry. Then she left the mirror for the reception hall to await their arrival, for it was time for them to be shown in.

The hall was a gem of art and architecture. It had been built by the architect Heni, who had designed an oval structure, constructing the walls of granite like the houses of the gods, and dressing them with a layer of flint, colored with delightful pigments. The ceiling was vaulted and adorned with pictures and intricate designs, and from it hung lamps embellished with silver and gold.

The sculptor Henfer had decorated the walls and her lovers had competed with one another to furnish it, presenting her with fine chairs, sumptuous couches, and beautiful feathers. Rhadopis's throne was the most wonderful of all these works of art, made from the richest ivory. Its legs were elephant tusks and its seat was of pure gold encrusted with emeralds and sapphires. It had been given to her by the governor of the island of Biga.

Rhadopis did not wait for long before one of her slaves entered and announced the arrival of Master Anin, the ivory merchant. The man entered immediately and rushed over in his flowing robes, proudly showing off his false hair. Behind him came a slave carrying a gilded ivory box. He set it down near the courtesan's chair and went out of the hall. The merchant bowed over Rhadopis's hand and kissed her fingertips. She smiled at him and said in her sweet voice, "Welcome, Master Anin. How are you? We really should see you more often. It has been so long."

The man laughed. He was delighted, and said, "What can I do, my lady? Such is the life I have chosen for myself, or which the Fates have decreed for me, that I should always be traveling the roads. A wanderer am I, hopping from country to country. I spend half the year in Nubia and the other half between the North and the South, buying and selling, selling and buying, always on the move."

She looked at the ivory box and still smiling asked, "What is this beautiful box? Could it be one of your precious gifts?"

"Not the box exactly, but rather what is inside it. It is from the tusk of a wild elephant. The Nubian trader I bought it from swore that four of his strongest men were killed trying to bring the beast down. I kept it in a safe place and never showed it to customers. Then when I rested up awhile in Tanis, I delivered it into the hands of the town's skilled craftsmen and they lined it with a layer of pure gold and gilded it on the outside so that it became a goblet fit only for kings to drink from. I said to myself, 'How fitting that this cup that has cost valuable lives should be given to her for whose sake no effort should be spared, if she would accept.'"

Rhadopis laughed politely and said, "Why thank you, Master Anin. Your gift, despite its great value, is not so beautiful as your words."

He was overjoyed and, staring at her with eyes full of admiration and yearning, said in a faint voice, "How beautiful you are, how ravishing. Every time I return from my travels I find you more ravishing and more beautiful than I left you. It seems to me as if time's only task is to enhance and magnify your unrivalled pulchritude."

She listened to him lauding her beauty as one listens to a familiar tune, and thinking she would enjoy a little sarcasm, she asked him, "How are your sons?"

He felt a twinge of disappointment and he was silent for a moment, then, bending over the box, he raised its lid. She could see the goblet resting on its side. "How biting your humor is, my lady," he said as he looked up at her. "And yet you will not find a single white hair on my head. Could anyone, having set eyes upon your face, retain in his heart the slightest affection for another woman?"

She did not answer but continued to smile. Then she invited him to be seated, and he sat down near to her. Immediately after, she received a group of merchants and land owners, some of whom frequented her palace every evening and others who she saw only at festivals and on special occasions, but she welcomed them all with her captivating smile. Then she espied the slim figure of the sculptor Henfer enter the hall with his tight curly hair and flat nose, and his Adam's apple protruding gently. He was one man whose company she enjoyed, and she extended her hand, which he kissed with deep affection.

"You lazy artist," she teased.

Henfer was not enamored of the description. "I finished my work in no time," he said.

"What about the summer room?"

"It is all that remains to be decorated. I'm afraid I have to tell you that I will not decorate it myself."

Rhadopis looked surprised.

"I am traveling to Nubia the day after tomorrow," Henfer explained. "My mother is sick and has sent a messenger requesting to see me. I have no alternative but to go."

"May the gods relieve her pain and yours."

Henfer thanked her and said, "Do not think I have forgotten the summer room. Tomorrow my most outstanding pupil, Benamun Ben Besar will come to see you. He will decorate it in the most beautiful fashion. I trust him as I trust myself. I trust you will welcome him and offer him your encouragement."

She thanked him for his kind attention and promised him she would do as he asked.

The stream of visitors continued. The architect Heni arrived, followed by Ani, the governor of the island, and a little while later, the poet Ramon Hotep. The last one to arrive was the philosopher Hof, who had until recently been the grand professor at the university in On, and who had returned to Abu, his place of birth, after reaching the age of seventy. Rhadopis was constantly teasing him. "Why is it that whenever I see you I want to kiss you?" she exclaimed.

"Perhaps, my lady, it is because you are fond of antiques," replied the philosopher dryly.

A group of slave girls entered carrying silver bowls filled with sweet perfume and garlands of lotus flowers, and they anointed the head, hands, and chest of each guest with perfume and gave him a lotus flower.

Rhadopis spoke in a loud voice, "Would you like to know what happened to me today?"

They all turned toward her eager to hear, and the hall fell silent. She smiled and said, "While I was bathing at noon today, a falcon swooped down and stole one of my golden sandals and flew away with it."

Smiles of surprise appeared on their faces, and the poet Ramon Hotep said, "Seeing you naked in the water has unhinged the birds of prey."

"I'll swear by Almighty Sothis that the falcon is wishing he had carried off the owner of the sandal instead," said Anin excitedly.

"It was so very dear to me," said Rhadopis sadly.

"It is truly distressing that something should be lost that has enjoyed your touch for days and weeks, and its only fate in the end will be to fall from the sky. Imagine if it falls into a remote field and a simple peasant's foot slips it on," said Henfer.

"Whatever its fate will be," said Rhadopis sadly, "I will never see it again."

The philosopher Hof was surprised to see Rhadopis so upset about a simple sandal, and he consoled her, saying, "In any case, the falcon carrying off your sandal is a good omen, so do not be sad."

"What happiness does Rhadopis lack when all these men are her lovers?" asked one of the guests, who was an important official.

Hof looked at him sternly. "She would be happier if she got rid of some of them," he said.

Another group of slave girls entered bearing jugs of wine and golden goblets. They moved among the throng, and wherever the signs of thirst appeared, they would pour the guest a brimming cup to slake the dryness in his mouth and fuel the fire in his heart. Rhadopis rose slowly to her feet, walked over to the ivory box, and held up the wonderful goblet. Then, holding it out to the slave who was bearing the wine, she said, "Let us drink a toast to Master Anin for his beautiful gift, and his safe return."

They all drank to the man's health. Anin emptied his cup in one swallow, and nodded to Rhadopis with a profound look of gratitude in his eyes. Then, turning to his friend, he said, "Is it not a most fortunate occurrence that the mention of my name should trip upon the tongue of Rhadopis?"

"Amen to that," said the man, at which point Governor

Ani, who knew Master Anin and had spotted him earlier, and knowing he had been in the South, said, "Welcome back Anin. How was your trip this time?"

Anin bowed respectfully, and said, "May the gods preserve you from every evil, my Lord Governor, this time I did not go beyond the region of Wawayu. It was a successful journey, most fruitful and rewarding."

"And how is His Excellency, Kaneferu, governor of the South?"

"The truth is that His Excellency is greatly vexed by the rebellion of the Maasayu tribes, for they harbor great hatred toward Egyptians. They lie in wait for them, and if they come upon a caravan, they attack it without mercy, kill the men, steal the goods, and then escape before the Egyptian forces can apprehend them."

The governor looked concerned and asked the merchant, "Why does His Excellency not send a punitive expedition against them?"

"His Excellency is always sending forces after them, but the tribes do not confront battle formations. They flee into the desert and the jungles and our troops are obliged to return to base when their supplies run out. Then the rebels resume their raids on the caravan routes."

The philosopher Hof listened to the words of Anin with great interest, for he had some experience of the land of Nubia and he was well acquainted with the Maasayu question.

"Why are the Maasayu always in revolt?" he inquired of the merchant. "Those lands under Egyptian rule enjoy peace and prosperity. We do not oppose the creeds of others. Why are they hostile to us?"

Anin was not concerned to know the reasons. He believed it was the value of the merchandise that tempted folk to swoop down upon it. Governor Ani, however, had made a thorough study of these matters. "The truth, esteemed professor," he said to the philosopher, "is that the Maasayu question has nothing to do with politics or religion. The reality of the matter is that they are nomadic tribes living in a desolate and barren land. They are threatened by starvation on occasion, and at the same time they possess treasures of gold and silver that cannot enrich them or fend off their hunger, and when the Egyptians undertake to put it to good use, they attack them and plunder their caravans."

"If that is the case," said Hof, "then punitive attacks are of no use. I recall, my Lord Governor, that Minister Una, may his soul be exalted in the realm of Osiris, at one time expended great effort to secure a treaty with them based on mutual benefit; he would provide them with food and they in return would guarantee the safety of the caravan routes. It seems a shrewd idea, does it not?"

The governor nodded his head in agreement.

"Prime Minister Khnumhotep resurrected Minister Una's plan and signed the treaty a few days before the festival of the Nile. We shall not know the results of his policy for a long time, though many are optimistic."

The guests soon tired of politics and split up into smaller groups, each one vying for Rhadopis's attention. She, however, had been intrigued by the name Khnumhotep and remembered the voice in the crowd that had shouted out his name earlier in the day. She felt the same shock and disapproval she had at that moment, and anger rose in her breast. She moved over to where Ani was sitting with Hof, Henfer, Heni, and Ramon Hotep. "Did you hear that amazing cry today?" she asked softly.

Those who frequented the white palace were brothers. No pretensions stood between them and no fear stayed their tongues. Their conversations broached every subject with the utmost candor and lack of inhibition. Hof had been heard criticizing the policies of the ministers many times, while Ramon Hotep had expressed his doubts and fears about the teaching of theology, openly declaring his epicurean beliefs, and calling for the enjoyment of worldly things.

Master Architect Heni drank a draught from his cup, and looking into Rhadopis's beautiful face, said, "It was a bold and audacious call, the like of which has not been heard in the Nile Valley before."

"Indeed," said Henfer. "No doubt it was a sad surprise to young Pharaoh so soon into his reign."

"It has never been the custom to call out a person's name, whatever his position might be, in the presence of Pharaoh," said Hof quietly.

"But they flaunted that custom so insolently," said Rhadopis, clearly outraged. "Why did they do that, my Lord Ani?"

Ani raised his thick eyebrows and said, "I suppose you ask what the people in the streets are saying. Many of the populace now know that Pharaoh wishes to appropriate a large portion of the clergy's estates for the crown and to ask for the return of the lavish grants showered on the men of the priesthood by his father and forebears."

"The clergy have always enjoyed the favor of the pharaohs," said Ramon Hotep in a tone not lacking in indignation. "Our rulers have bestowed lands upon the priests and have given them money; the theocrats now own a third of all the agricultural land in the kingdom. Their influence has spread to the remotest regions and all and sundry are held in their sway. Surely there are causes more deserving of money than the temples?"

"The priests claim they spend the income from their estates on works of charity and piety," said Hof. "And they are always declaring that they would gladly relinquish their properties if necessity required them to do so."

"And what might such a necessity be?"

"If the kingdom were to be embroiled in a war, for example, that required great expenditure."

Rhadopis thought for a moment. "Even so, they cannot oppose the wishes of the king," she said.

"They are making a serious mistake," said Governor Ani. "And what is more, they have been sending their representatives throughout the regions putting it into the minds of the peasants that they, the priesthood, are defending the sacred property of the gods."

Rhadopis was astonished. "How do they have the nerve?"

"The country is at peace," said Ani. "The royal guard are the only armed force to be reckoned with. That is why they have the nerve, for they know very well that Pharaoh's forces are not sufficient to contain them."

Rhadopis was irate. "What vile people," she said furiously.

Hof, the philosopher, smiled. He was never one to keep his opinion to himself. "If you want the truth, the priesthood is a pure and unsullied institution that watches over the religion of this nation, and preserves its eternal mores and traditions. As for the lusting after power, it is an ancient malady."

The poet Ramon Hotep, ever fond of provoking controversy, glared at him. "And Khnumhotep?" he demanded of the philosopher angrily.

Hof shrugged his shoulders in disdain. "He is a priest as he should be, and a clever politician. No one would deny that he is strong-willed and extremely shrewd," he said with his extraordinary calmness.

Governor Ani mumbled to himself, shaking his head with some intensity. "He has yet to prove his loyalty to the throne."

"He has announced the very opposite," exclaimed Rhadopis angrily.

The philosopher did not agree with them. "I know Khnumhotep well. His loyalty to Pharaoh and the realm is beyond reproach."

"All that remains, then, is for you to declare that Pharaoh is mistaken," said Ani incredulously.

"I would not dream of it. Pharaoh is a young man with high hopes. He wishes to dress his country in a garment of splendor, and that will not come about unless he makes use of some of the priesthood's resources."

"So who is mistaken then?" asked Ramon Hotep, confused.

"Is it not possible that two people disagree and both are right?" said Hof.

But Rhadopis was not happy with the philosopher's explanation, and she did not like the comparison he had made between the Pharaoh and his minister, implying that they were equals. She believed in an unshakeable truth: that Pharaoh was sole master of the land, with none to contend with him, and that no one could question him whatever the reason or circumstance. In her heart, she rejected any opinion that contradicted her belief. She announced this opinion to her friends and then concluded, "I wonder when it was that I came to hold this opinion?"

"When you first set eyes on Pharaoh," said Ramon Hotep playfully. "Do not be so surprised, for beauty is just as convincing as the truth."

The sculptor Henfer grew restless and called out, "Slave girls! Fill the cups. And Rhadopis, enchantress, let us hear a moving melody, or delight our eyes with a graceful dance. For our souls are merry with the wine of Maryut and the festival has put us in the mood for pleasure and joy. We are longing for rapturous entertainment and saucy indulgence."

Rhadopis paid him no heed. She wanted to continue the conversation but when she noticed Anin the merchant seemingly asleep on his own, away from the clusters of revelers, she realized she had tarried too long with Ani's group, and she stood up and walked over to the merchant.

"Wake up," she shouted in his face. The man jolted to attention, but his face soon lit up when he saw her. She sat down next to him and asked, "Were you asleep?"

"Indeed I was, and dreaming too."

"Ah. What about?"

"About the happy nights of Biga. And in my confusion I was wondering if I would ever win one of those immortal unforgettable nights. If only I could obtain a promise from you now."

She shook her head. He was taken aback, and cautiously, nervously, he asked her, "Why not?"

"My heart may desire you, or it may desire someone else. I do not bind it with false promises."

She left him and moved over to another group. They were deep in conversation and drink. They welcomed her loudly and gathered round her from every side.

"Would you join in our conversation?" asked one of them, whose name was Shama.

"What are you talking about?"

"Some of us were wondering whether artists deserve the recognition and honor that the pharaohs and ministers bestow upon them."

"And have you reached any agreement?"

"Yes, my lady, that they do not deserve anything."

Shama was speaking in a loud voice, unconcerned who could hear. Rhadopis looked over to where the artists were sitting: Ramon Hotep, Henfer, and Heni, and she laughed mischievously, a sweet enchanting laugh, and in a voice loud enough for the artists to hear, she said, "This conversation should be open to everyone. Do you not hear, gentlemen, what is being said about you? They are saying here that art is a trivial pursuit and that artists are not worthy of the honor and recognition they receive. What do you have to say?"

A sly smile appeared on the old philosopher's lips, while the artists looked haughtily across at the group that had so contemptuously disdained their calling. Henfer smiled arrogantly, while Ramon Hotep's face went yellow with anger, for he was easily provoked. Shama was happy to repeat what he had been saying to his friends in a louder voice for all to hear.

"I am a man of action and resolve. I strike the earth with a hand of iron, and it is humbled, and gives freely to me of its bounty and abundant blessings, and I benefit and thousands of other needy people benefit with me. All this happens without any need for measured words or brilliant colors."

Each man spoke his mind, either to let out some ill will he had long harbored in his mind, or simply to chatter and give voice to his thoughts. One of the more important guests, whose name was Ram, said, "Who is it that rules and guides the people? Who conquers new lands and storms fortresses? Who is it that brings in wealth and profit? It is certainly not the artists."

"Men are passionately in love with women," announced Anin, who was quick to fill his glass at every opportunity, "and they rave about them inanely. Poets, however, couch this ranting in well-balanced words. No reasonable person would hold them to account for that, except perhaps that they should waste their time in something so futile and ephemeral. The ridiculous thing is that they should demand some fame or glory in exchange for their ranting."

Shama spoke again, "Others tell long prosodic lies or wander in raptures through distant valleys seeking inspiration from phantoms and vain imaginings, claiming they are messengers with revelation. Children tell lies too, and many of the common folk, but they do not claim anything in return."

Rhadopis laughed a long and hearty laugh, and moved over to where Henfer was sitting. "Shame on you artists," she mocked. "Why then do you walk proud and conceited, as if you have grown as tall as the mountains?"

The sculptor smiled condescendingly but remained silent like his two companions, deeming himself above a response to those who attack without knowledge, while Ramon Hotep and Heni both contained their rising anger. Unwilling to see the battle end at this point, Rhadopis turned to Hof, the philosopher. "What do you think, philosopher, of art and artists?" she asked him.

"Art is entertainment and jest, and artists are skillful jesters."

The artists were unable to conceal their anger, and Governor Ani could not contain his laughter. A roar of delight went up from the guests.

"My dear philosopher, do you want life to be simple drudgery and nothing else?" cried Ramon Hotep angrily.

The old man shook his head calmly, and with the smile still upon his lips, said, "Not at all. That was not my intention. Jest is necessary, but we should bear in mind that it is jest."

"Is inspired creativity jest?" challenged Henfer.

"You call it inspiration and creativity," said the philosopher dismissively. "I know it is the play of fantasy."

Rhadopis looked at Heni, the architect, urging him to join in the fray, endeavoring to bring him out of his usual silence, but the man did not succumb to her temptation, not because he held that matter in question to be of little value, but because he believed, rightly or wrongly, that Hof did not mean what he was saying, and was teasing Henfer, and Ramon Hotep in particular, in his cruel manner. The poet, on the other hand, was greatly angered, and forgetting for a moment that he was in the palace of Biga, he addressed the philosopher in a spiteful tone: "If art is the play of fantasy then why are artists commissioned to do things they have not the capacity to achieve?"

"Because it demands of them to put aside the thought and logic they are used to and to seek refuge in a world of childhood and fantasy."

The poet shrugged his shoulders disdainfully. "Your words do not deserve a response," he said.

"Amen," said Henfer, and Heni smiled in agreement, but Ramon Hotep had grown impatient and his anger would not allow him to be silent. He glared at the mocking faces, and said vehemently, "Does not art create pleasure and beauty for you?"

"How trivial that is," said Anin, who hardly knew what he was saying for the wine had fuddled his mind.

The poet was furious. He let the lotus flower fall from his hand. "What is wrong with these people?" he blurted out. "They do not understand the meaning of what they are saying. Is it possible that I can mention pleasure and beauty and be told that they are trivial things? Is there then no purpose in the world to pleasure and beauty?"

Henfer was pleased with his companion's words and a flush of excitement came over him. He leaned over to Rhadopis's ear. "Your beauty is true, Rhadopis," he said. "Life passes like a swiftly unfolding dream. I remember, for example, how sad I was at my father's death, and how bitterly I wept. But now whenever his memory comes to me I ask myself, 'Did this person really live upon the earth or was he just an illusion appearing to me in the twilight?' That is life. What benefit accrues to the mighty and powerful from their achievements, what gains to those who produce wealth and riches? What have rulers acquired from their ruling and leading? Are not their achievements like dust scattered in the wind? Power could be folly, wisdom error, and wealth vanity. As for pleasure, it is pleasure, it can be nothing else. Everything that is not beauty is worthless."

A grave look appeared on Rhadopis's enchanting face, and dreams glimmered in her eyes as she said, "Who knows, Henfer, perhaps pleasure and beauty are trivialities too. Do you not see how I live my life in gentle comfort, courting pleasure, enjoying goodness and beauty? And yet despite all that, how often I am dogged by boredom and dejection."

Rhadopis could see that Ramon Hotep was in a bad mood, and as she considered Henfer's displeasure and Heni's silence, she was touched by their hurt, and feeling responsible, she decided it was time to change the subject. "Gentlemen, enough! Whatever you have said, you shall never cease to search out art and seek the company of artists. You love them, though you relish in attacking them. You would make happiness itself a subject of debate and controversy."

Governor Ani had grown weary of the discussion. "Dispel the dissenters with one of your happy songs," he suggested.

Everyone longed to listen and enjoy, and they were united in their vociferous support of the governor's request. Rhadopis agreed. She had had enough of conversation and she felt once again the strange apprehension that had come over her several times that day. She thought that a song or a dance would drive it away, and, stepping over to her throne, she summoned her songstresses, who came with drums, lyres, flutes, and a wang and pipes, and lined up behind her.

Rhadopis gave a signal with her ivory hand and all began to play a beautiful rhythm and a graceful beat, providing a gorgeous musical accompaniment to her melodious voice. The musicians softened the sounds of their instruments and they became like the whispers of starry-eyed lovers, as Rhadopis began to sing the ode of Ramon Hotep:

> *O ye who listen to the sermons of the wise, lend me your ears, I have seen the world since the beginning of time, the passing of your forebears, who came and alighted here awhile like thoughts alight on the mind of a dreaming man. I have had my fill of laughing at their promises and threats. Where are the pharaohs, where are the politicians, where are the vanquishing heroes? Is the grave truly the threshold of eternity? No messenger has returned thence to put our hearts at rest, so do not shun pleasure, and do not let earthly delights pass you by, for the voice of her who pours the wine is more eloquently wise than the shrieking of the preacher.*

The courtesan sang the words with a serene and tender voice, liberating the listeners' souls from the shackles of the body to float in the welkin of beauty and joy, mindless of worldly troubles and the cares of this life, partaking of the most sublime mystery. And when she stopped, the guests remained enraptured, sighing sighs of joy and sadness, pleasure and pain.

Love drove all other emotions from their breasts and they vied in drinking, their eyes transfixed on the gorgeous woman who tripped lightly through their midst, flirting with them, teasing them, supping with them. And when she came to Ani, he whispered in her ear, "May the gods bring you happiness, Rhadopis. I came to you a shadow of myself, weighed down with woes, and now I feel like a bird soaring in the sky."

She smiled at him and then moved over to Ramon Hotep and offered him a lotus flower to replace the one he had lost. "This old man says that art is jest and fantasy," he said to her. "I say, to hell with his opinion. Art is that divine spark of light that flashes in your eyes, and, resounding in harmony with the throbbing of my heart, works miracles."

Rhadopis laughed. "What do I do that causes miracles to happen? I am more powerless than a suckling child."

Then she hurried over to where Hof was sitting and sat down next to him. He had not tasted the wine and as she looked at him seductively, he laughed and said sarcastically, "What a poor choice of one to sit with."

"Do you not love me like the rest of them do?"

"If only I could. But I find in you that which a cold man finds in a burning stove."

"Then advise me what I should do with my life, for today I am sorely troubled."

"Are you really troubled? With all this luxury and wealth you complain?"

"How could it have escaped you, O Wise One?"

"Everyone complains, Rhadopis. How often I have heard the bitter grumbling of the poor and the wretched who yearn for a crust of bread. How often I have listened to the bellyaching of rulers who groan under the weight of enormous responsibilities. How many times I have listened to the whining of the rich and reckless who have tired of wealth and luxury. Everyone complains, so what is the use of hoping for change? Be content with your lot."

"Do people complain in the realm of Osiris?"

The old man smiled. "Aah. Your friend Ramon Hotep scoffs at that exalted world while the scholar priests tell us it is the eternal abode. Be patient, beautiful woman, for you are still little experienced."

The wave of dalliance and sarcasm came over her again, and she thought to tease the philosopher. "Do you really think I have little experience?" she said, feigning a serious tone. "You have seen nothing of the things I have seen."

"And what have you seen that I have not?"

She pointed to the drunken throng and laughed. "I have seen these outstanding men, the cream of Egypt, mistress of the world, prostrating themselves at my feet. They have reverted to a state of barbarism, and forgotten their wisdom and dignity, they are like dogs or monkeys."

She laughed delicately, and with the agility of a gazelle she stepped into the center of the hall. She signaled to her musicians and their fingers plucked the strings, as the courtesan danced one of her select dances at which her lithe and lissome body excelled, working miracles of nimbleness and flexibility. The guests were absorbed in the entertainment, and clapped their hands in time to the drums, a subtle fire smoldering in their eyes, and when she ended her dance, she flew like a dove back to her throne, whereupon she cast her eyes round their greedy faces. The sight made her roar with laughter: "It is as if I am among wolves."

Anin, in his drunken state, relished the comparison, and he wished he were a wolf so that he might pounce on the beautiful ewe. The wine made his wish come true, and thinking he was really a wolf, he let out a great howl and the guests roared with laughter. But he went on howling and got down on all fours, and crawled toward Rhadopis amidst the uproarious laughter until he was only inches away from her. "Make this night belong to me," he said.

She did not reply, but rather turned to Governor Ani, who had come to bid her farewell, and extended her hand. Philosopher Hof came next. "Would you like this night to belong to you?" she asked him.

He shook his head and laughed. "It would be easier to make jokes with the prisoners of war who labor in the mines of Koptos."

Each man wanted the night to belong to him, and eagerly demanded so, and they competed vehemently until matters were almost out of hand, at which point Henfer took it upon himself to find a solution. "Let each of you write his name on a paper, and let us put the names in Anin's ivory casket, then Rhadopis may draw out the name of the lucky winner."

They were all obliged to agree and they quickly wrote down their names, except for Anin, who saw his chances of the night receding. "My lady," he beseeched, "I am a man of travel. Today I am here before you, tomorrow in a far-off land reached only with great effort. If this night passes me by I might lose it forever."

His defense infuriated the guests and was greeted with hoots of derision. Rhadopis was silent as she surveyed her lovers with cold eyes. A strange apprehension came over her and she felt a desire to flee and be alone. She was tired of the din and she raised her hand. They fell silent as they stood suspended between hope and fear. "Do not tire yourselves, gentlemen. Tonight I shall belong to no man."

Openmouthed they gazed at her, unwilling to acknowledge her words, unable to believe their ears, then they burst into shouts of protest and complaint. She realized there was no point in talking to them and she stood up, a look of determination and resolve upon her face. "I am tired. Please allow me to rest."

And with a wave of her tender hand she turned her back on them and hurried out of the room.

As she went up to her bedchamber, the heated protests of the men still ringing in her ears, she felt delighted at what she had done, and great relief that she had been spared that night. She hurried straight over to the window and drew aside the curtain, and looking out at the dark road, she saw the shapes of chariots and litters in the distance carrying her drunken guests off into the night as they nursed their grief and disappointment. She relished the sight of them and a cruel and malicious smile formed upon her lips.

How had she done it? She did not know, but she felt uneasy, nervous. "O Lord," she sighed, "what is the point of this monotonous life?" The answer evaded her. Not even the wise man Hof had been able to quench her burning thirst. She lay down on her sumptuous bed and went over the day's strange and wonderful events one by one in her mind. She saw the throngs of Egyptians and the burning eyes of the sorceress, which had seemed to hold her own eyes with an overpowering force, and she heard the crone's repulsive voice and her joints shivered. Then she saw the young pharaoh in all his finery, and next, that magnificent falcon who had flown off with her sandal. It had indeed been an eventful day. Perhaps that is what had roused her emotions and distracted her thoughts, shattering her into so many pieces. Her unfortunate lovers had paid the price for that. Her heart thumped loudly and burned with a mysterious flame, and her imagination roamed through unfamiliar valleys, as if she longed to pass from this state into another. But what state was it? She was baffled, unable to comprehend what was happening to her. Could it have been a waft of magic sent out to her by that accursed sorceress?

She was obviously under a spell, and if it was not the spell of a witch, then it was the spell of the Fates that control all destinities.

Tahu

Anxious and troubled with all kinds of disturbing thoughts, she despaired of ever finding sleep. She rose from her bed once again, walked slowly over to the window, and throwing it wide open, stood there like a statue. She undid the clasp that held her hair and it flowed in shimmering tresses over her neck and shoulders, touching the whiteness of her gown with a deep black. She breathed the damp night air into her lungs and put her elbows onto the window ledge, resting her chin in the palms of her hands. Her eyes wandered over the garden to the Nile flowing beyond the walls. It was a mild dark night, a gentle intermittent breeze was blowing and the leaves and branches danced discreetly. The Nile could be seen in the distance like a patch of blackness and the sky was adorned with shining stars that emitted a pale radiance that almost drowned in seas of darkness just as it reached the earth.

Would the dark night and the overwhelming silence be able to cast a shade of stillness and relief over her troubled mind? Alas, she felt as if her mind would never be at rest again. She fetched a pillow and placed it on the window sill and laid her right cheek upon it and closed her eyes.

Suddenly the words of Hof, the philosopher, came back to her: "Everyone complains, so what is the use of hoping for change? Be content with your lot." She sighed from the depths of her heart, and asked herself dolefully, "Is there really no use hoping for change? Will people always complain?" But how was she to believe this so completely that it would sway her own heart from desiring change? A storm of defiance was brewing in her breast. She wanted it to sweep away her present and her past and she would escape to find salvation in lands mysterious and unknown beyond the horizon. How would she ever find conviction and peace of mind? She was dreaming of a state where there would be no need to grieve, but she was apprehensive, weary of all things.

She was not to be left to her thoughts and dreams though, for she heard a gentle knock on the door of her chamber. She pricked up her ears in surprise and lifted her head off the pillow.

"Who is it?" she called.

"It is I, my lady," replied a familiar voice. "May I enter?"

"Come in Shayth," said Rhadopis.

The slave girl came in on the tips of her toes. She was surprised to find her mistress still up, and her bed unslept in.

"What is it, Shayth?" Rhadopis inquired.

"A man is here who awaits permission to enter."

Rhadopis frowned and could barely conceal her anger. "What man? Throw him out without delay."

"How, my lady? He is a man the door of this palace is never closed to."

"Tahu?"

"Yes, it is he."

"And what has brought him at this late hour of the night?"

A mischievous glint flashed in the woman's eye. "That you will know soon enough, my lady."

With a wave of her hand, Rhadopis signaled her to call him, and the slave girl disappeared. A moment later the commander's tall, broad figure filled the doorway. He greeted her with a bow then stood before her, looking at her face in confusion. She could not help noticing his pale color and furrowed brow, and the darkness in his eyes. She ignored him and walked over to the divan and sat down. "You look tired. Is your work wearing you out?" she asked him.

He shook his head. "No," he said curtly.

"You do not look your usual self."

"Is that so?"

"You must know that. What is the matter with you?"

He knew everything, no doubt about it, and she would know in a moment, whether he told her himself or not. He was wary of being so audacious as to speak, because he was risking his happiness and he was afraid she would slip through his hands and be lost to him forever. If he were able to prevail over her will, everything would be so easy, but he had almost given up hope of that, and was tormented by pangs of anguish.

"Ah, Rhadopis! If only you felt for me the love I feel for you, then I could beseech you in the name of our love."

She wondered why he needed to beseech. She had always considered him an aggressive man who detested beseeching and pleading. He had always been satisfied with the charm and enticement of her body. What was it that had upset him? She lowered her eyes. "It is the same old talk as before."

Her words, though they were true, still angered him. "I know that," he shouted. "But I am repeating it for reasons of the present. Ah, your heart is like an empty cavern at the bottom of an icy river."

She was familiar with such comparisons, but her words

twitched nervously as she spoke. "Have I ever refused to give you what you wanted?"

"Never Rhadopis. You have granted me your enchanting body, which was created to torment mankind. But I have always yearned for your heart. What a heart it is, Rhadopis. It stands firm and steadfast amidst the stormy tempests of passion as if it does not belong to you. How often I have asked myself in confusion and exasperation, what faults do mar me? Is it that I am not a man? Nay, for I am the very paragon of manhood. The truth is that you do not have a heart."

She wanted nothing to do with him. It was not the first time she had heard these words, but normally he spoke them with sarcasm or some mild anger. Now, at this late hour of the night, he was speaking with a shaking voice full of fury and resentment. What could have inflamed him so? To elicit an explanation she asked him, "Have you come at this late hour of the night, Tahu, to simply repeat these words in my ears?"

"No, I have not come for the sake of these words. I have come for a far more serious matter, and if love fails to help me in its regard, then let your freedom assist me, for it seems you are keen to hold on to that."

She looked at him curiously, and waited for him to speak. He could stand the tension no longer and, determined to get to the point without further delay, he addressed her quietly and firmly as he looked straight into her eyes. "You should leave the palace of Biga, and escape from the island as soon as possible, before dawn breaks."

Rhadopis was stunned. She looked at him with disbelief in her eyes. "What are you saying, Tahu?"

"I am saying that you should disappear, or else you will lose your freedom."

"And what threatens my freedom on Biga?"

He ground his teeth, and then asked her, "Have you not lost something valuable?"

"Why yes. I lost one of the golden sandals you gave to me."

"How?"

"A falcon snatched it away while I was bathing in the garden pool. But I do not understand what a lost sandal has to do with my threatened freedom."

"Slowly, Rhadopis. The falcon carried it off, that is true, but do you know where it landed?"

She could tell from the way he spoke that he knew the answer. She was astonished. "How should I know that, Tahu?" she muttered.

He sighed, "It landed in Pharaoh's lap."

His words echoed ominously in her ears and pervaded all her senses. All else faded from her mind. She looked at Tahu with confusion in her eyes, unable to utter a sound. The commander scrutinized her face with nervous and suspicious eyes. He wondered how she had taken the news, and what feelings surged in her breast. He could not contain himself and asked her softly, "Was I not right in my request?"

She did not reply. She did not seem to be listening to him. She was drowning in a storm of confusion and the waves crashed against her heart. Her stillness filled him with fear, and her confusion was almost too much for him to bear, for he read into it meanings that his heart refused to acknowledge. At length his patience ran out and his anger put him on the defensive. His eyes narrowed as he roared at her, "Which valley are you lost in now, woman? Does this terrible news not alarm you?"

Her body trembled at the power in his voice, and anger

blazed in her heart. She glared at him with hatred in her eyes, but she suppressed her rage, for she was going to get her own way. "Is that how you see it?" she asked him coldly.

"I see that you are pretending not to understand what this means, Rhadopis."

"How unjust you are. What does it matter if the sandal landed in Pharaoh's lap. Do you think he will kill me for it?"

"Of course not. But he held the sandal in his hands and asked who the owner might be."

Rhadopis felt a flutter in her heart. "Did he receive an answer?" she asked.

Tahu's eyes misted over. "There was a person there waiting for a chance to confound me," he said. "The Fates have made him friend and foe at one and the same time. He snatched the opportunity and stabbed me in the back, for he mentioned your enchanting beauty to Pharaoh, sowing the seed of desire in his heart and igniting passion in his breast."

"Sofkhatep?"

"The very same, that enemy-friend. He stirred temptation in the young king's heart."

"And what does the king want to do?"

Tahu crossed his arms over his chest, and spoke loudly, "Pharaoh is not a person who just desires a thing when it is dear to him. If he loves something, he knows how to take it for himself."

Silence fell once again, the woman falling prey to burning emotions while the nightmare settled in the man's breast. His anger grew at her reticence, and because she was not alarmed or afraid.

"Do you not see that this threatens to curtail your freedom?" he said furiously. "Your freedom, Rhadopis, which you are so eager to preserve, and care about so much. Your freedom, which has destroyed hearts and devastated so many souls, and which has made anguish, grief, and despair plagues that have smitten every man on Biga. Why are you not afraid to stay here and lose it?"

She disapproved of the way he was describing her freedom and she vented her indignation. "Would you hurl such vile accusations at me when my only fault is that I have not allowed myself to be a hypocrite and tell a man falsely that I love him?"

"And why do you not love, Rhadopis? Even Tahu, the mighty warrior, who has fearlessly plunged into the hazards of war in the South and the North, who was raised on the backs of chariots, has loved. Why do you not love?"

She smiled mysteriously. "I wonder if I possess an answer to your question?" she asked.

"I do not care about that now. That is not why I came. I am asking you what you are going to do."

"I do not know," she said quietly and with astonishing resignation.

His eyes glowed like hot coals, consuming her in a fury. He felt a mad urge to smash her head into pieces, then suddenly she looked at him and he sighed deeply. "I thought you would be more jealous of your freedom."

"And what do you suggest I should do?"

He clasped his hands together. "Escape, Rhadopis. Escape before you are carried off to the ruler's palace as a slave girl to be placed in one of his countless rooms where you would live in isolated servitude, waiting your turn once a year, spending the rest of your life in a sad paradise that is really a miserable prison. Were you created, Rhadopis, to live such a life?"

She revolted furiously at the thought of such an affront to her dignity and pride, and wondered if it might really be her misfortune to live such a miserable life.

Would it really be her destiny in the end—she, to whom the cream of Egypt's manhood flocked to woo—to compete with slave girls for the young pharaoh's affection, and content herself with a room in the royal harem? Did she want darkness after light, to be enveloped in destitution after glory, to be satisfied with bondage after complete and utter mastery? Alas, what an abominable thought, an unimaginable eventuality. But would she flee as Tahu wished? Would she be happy with flight? Would Rhadopis, whom they worshipped, whose beauty no other face possessed, and with whose magic no other body was endowed, flee from slavery? Who, then, would crave mastery and power over men's hearts?

Tahu stepped closer. "Rhadopis, what are you saying?" he implored.

She was angry again. "Are you not ashamed, Commander, to incite me to flee from the countenance of your lord?" she mocked.

Her biting sarcasm struck him deep in his heart, and he reeled from the shock. "My lord has not seen you yet, Rhadopis," he blurted as he felt the bitterness rise in his throat. "As for me, my heart was wrested from me long ago. I am a prisoner of a turbulent love that knows no mercy, that leads me only to ruin and perdition, trampled under the feet of shame and degradation. My breast is a furnace of torment which burns more fiercely at the thought of losing you forever. If then I urge you to flee, it is to defend my love, and not to betray His Sacred Majesty at all."

She paid no heed to his complaints, nor to his protestations of loyalty to his lord. She was still angry for her pride, and so when he asked her what she intended to do, she shook her head violently as if to dislodge the malicious whisperings that had taken hold there, and in a cold voice full of confidence, she said, "I will not flee, Tahu."

The man stood there, grave faced, astonished, desperate. "Are you to be content with ignominy, prepared to accept humiliation?"

"Rhadopis will never taste humiliation," she said with a smile on her lips.

Tahu was fuming. "Ah, I understand now. Your old devil has stirred. That devil of vanity and pride and power, that protects itself with the eternal coldness of your heart and relishes to see the pain and torment of others, and sits in judgment of men's fates. It heard Pharaoh's name and rebelled, and now it wishes to test its strength and power, and to prove the supremacy of its accursed beauty, without regard for the crippled hearts and broken spirits and shattered dreams it leaves in its demonic wake. Ah, why do I not put an end to this evil with a single thrust of this dagger?"

She regarded him with a look of composure in her eyes. "I have never denied you anything, and always have I warned you about temptation."

"This dagger will suffice to calm my soul. What a fitting end it would be for Rhadopis."

"What a sorry end it would be for Tahu, commander of the royal forces," she said calmly.

His hard eyes looked at her for a long time. He felt, at that decisive moment, a sense of mortal despair and stifling loss, but he did not allow his anger to get the better of him, and in a cruel cold voice he said, "How ugly you are, Rhadopis. How repulsive and twisted an image you display. Whomever thinks you beautiful is blind, without vision. You are ugly because you are dead, and there is no beauty without life. Life has never flowed through your veins. Your heart has never been warm. You are a corpse with perfect features, but a corpse nevertheless. Compassion has not shone in your eyes, your lips have never parted in pain, nor has your heart felt pity. Your eyes are hard and your heart is made of stone. You are a corpse, damn you! I should hate you, and rue the day I ever loved you. I know well that you will dominate and control wherever your devil wishes you to. But one day you will be brought crashing to the ground, your soul shattered into many pieces. That is the end of everything. Why should I kill you then? Why should I carry the burden of murdering a corpse that is already dead?"

With these words Tahu departed.

Rhadopis listened to his heavy footfall until the silence of the night enveloped her. Then she went back to the window. The darkness was absolute and the stars looked down from their eternal banquet, and in the solemn all-encompassing silence, she thought she could hear secrets fluttering deep in her heart.

There was a power in her, violent with heat and unrest. She was alive, her body throbbing with life, not a dead corpse.

Pharaoh

She opened her eyes and saw darkness. It must still be night. How many hours had she been able to find sleep and tranquility? For a few moments she was not aware of anything at all, she could remember nothing, as if the past was unknown to her just as the future is unknown, and the pitch-black night had consumed her identity. For a while she felt bewildered and weary, but then her eyes grew used to the dark and she could perceive a faint light creeping in through the curtains. She could make out the shapes of the furniture and she saw the hanging lamp coated in gold. Her senses suddenly became sharper and she remembered that she had remained awake, her eyelids not tasting sleep until the gentle blue waves of dawn washed over her. Then she had lain on her bed and sleep had carried her away from her emotions and her dreams. If that were so, it would be well into the next day, or even its evening.

She recalled the events of the previous night. The image of Tahu came back to her, fuming and raging, groaning with despair, threatening hatred and abomination. What a violent man he was, a bully with a brutal temper, madly infatuated. His only fault was that his love was stubborn and persistent, and he was deeply smitten. She sincerely hoped he would forget her or despise her. All she ever gained from love was pain. Everyone yearned for her heart and her heart remained unapproachable and aloof, like an untamed animal. How often she had been forced to plunge into disturbing scenarios and painful tragedies even though she hated it. But tragedy had followed her like a shadow, hovering around her like her deepest thoughts, spoiling her life with its cruelty and pain.

Then she remembered what Tahu had said about young Pharaoh and how he had desired to see the woman the sandal belonged to, and that he would summon her eventually to join his thriving harem. Ah, Pharaoh was a young man with fire in his blood and impetuosity in his mind, or so she had been told. It was no wonder Tahu had said what he had, and it was not impossible to believe it either, but she wondered whether events might not take a different course. Her faith in herself knew no bounds.

She heard a knock at the door. "Shayth," she called lazily. "Come in."

The slave opened the door and, stepping into the room with her familiar nimble gait, said, "Lord have mercy on you, my lady. You must be famished."

Shayth opened the window. The light that came in was already fading. "The sun went down today without seeing you," she laughed. "He wasted his journey to the earth."

"Is it evening?" asked Rhadopis, stretching and yawning.

"Yes, my lady. Now, are you going to the perfumed water, or would you like to eat? It's a pity, but I know what kept you awake last night."

"What was it, Shayth?" asked Rhadopis with interest.

"You did not warm your bed with a man."

"Stop it, you wicked woman."

"Men are always so forceful, my lady," said the slave with a glint in her eye. "Otherwise you would never put up with their vanity."

"Enough of your nonsense, Shayth," she said, then complained of a sore head.

"Let us go to the bath," said Shayth. "Your admirers are starting to assemble in the reception hall, and it pains them to see you are not there."

"Have they really come?"

"Has the reception hall ever been empty of them at this hour?"

"I will not see a single one of them."

Shayth's face went pale, and she looked at her mistress suspiciously. "You disappointed them yesterday. What will you say today? If only you knew how anxious they are at your tardiness."

"Tell them I am not well."

The slave girl hesitated, and was about to object, but Rhadopis yelled at her, "Do as I say!"

The woman left the bedchamber in a fluster, wondering what had brought such a change over her mistress.

Rhadopis was pleased with her response. She told herself that this was not the time for lovers, and in any case she could not muster her scattered thoughts to listen to anyone, nor form her ideas into any conversation, let alone dance or sing. Let them all be off. Still, she was afraid that Shayth would return with pleas and protestations from the guests and she got off the bed and hurried to the bathroom.

Inside and alone, she wondered if Pharaoh would send for her that very evening. Yes, that was why she was so nervous and confused. Perhaps even afraid? But no. Such beauty as hers, that no woman had ever possessed, was enough to fill her with boundless self-confidence. That is how she was. No man would resist her beauty. Her gorgeous looks would not be debased for a single soul, even if it were Pharaoh himself. But then why was she nervous and confused? The strange feeling came back to her, the one she had felt the previous night, and which she had first felt throb in her heart when she set eyes upon the young pharaoh as he stood like a statue in the back of his chariot. How magnificent he was! She wondered if she were confused because she stood before an enigma, an awesome and omnipotent name, a god worshipped by all. Was it because she wished to see him a passionate human being after she had beheld him in all his divine glory, or was she nervous because she wanted to be assured of her power in the face of this impregnable fortress?

Shayth knocked on the bathroom door, and informed her that Master Anin had sent with her a letter for her lady. Rhadopis was furious and told Shayth to tear it up.

The slave girl feared to incur her mistress's anger and she stumbled out of the room in disarray. Rhadopis emerged from the bathroom into the bedchamber, stunningly beautiful, flawlessly attired. She ate her food and drank a cup of fine vintage Maryut. But hardly had she relaxed on her couch than Shayth came running into the room without knocking. Rhadopis glared at her. "There is a strange man in the hall. He insists on meeting you," said the frightened slave.

"Have you gone completely mad?" cried Rhadopis in anger. "Have you joined forces against me with that bunch of tiresome men?"

"Be patient a moment, my lady," urged Shayth as she gasped for breath. "I showed out all the guests. This man is a stranger. I have not set eyes on him before. I stumbled upon him in the corridor leading to the hall. I do not know where he came from. I tried to block his way but he would not be swayed. He ordered me to inform you of his request."

Rhadopis looked gravely at her slave for a moment. "Is he an officer from the royal guard?" she asked with interest.

"No, mistress. He does not wear the uniform of an officer. I asked him to tell me who he was, but he just shrugged his shoulders. I insisted you would not be receiving anyone today but he set little store by my words. He ordered me to inform you that he was waiting. Oh dear, my lady. I would have you think well of me, but he was insistent and audacious. I could find no way to deter him."

She wondered if it was an emissary from the king. Her heart missed a beat at the very thought, and her chest heaved. She ran to the mirror and inspected herself, then she twirled on the tips of her toes, her face still fixed on the mirror. "What do you see, Shayth?" she asked the slave.

"I see Rhadopis, my lady," replied Shayth, amazed at the change that had come over her mistress.

Rhadopis left the bedchamber, leaving her bewildered slave in a daze. She floated like a dove from room to room and then descended the stairs, which were covered in sumptuous carpets. Then, pausing a moment at the entrance to the hall, she spotted a man with his back to her, his face toward the wall as he read the poetry of Ramon Hotep. Who could it be? He was as tall as Tahu but slimmer and more delicate, broad shouldered, with beautiful legs. Across his back was a sash encrusted with jewels hanging down between his shoulders as far as his waist, and on his head he wore a beautiful tall helmet in the shape of a pyramid that did not look like the headgear of the priests. Who was it? He did not know she was there because her feet made no noise on the thick carpet. When she was only a few steps from him, she said, "My lord?"

The stranger turned to look at her.

"O Lord," she gasped, as she realized she was standing face-to-face with Pharaoh. Pharaoh himself in all his divine glory. Merenra the Second, none other.

The surprise shook her to the core and she was totally overcome. She thought for a second it might be a dream, but there was no mistaking the dark face, the fine proud nose. She could never forget him. She had seen him twice before and he had found his way into her memory and engraved upon its tablet deep impressions that would never fade. But she had not reckoned on this meeting. She had not prepared for it or drawn up one of her ingenious plans. Here was Rhadopis meeting Pharaoh, completely out of the blue, when she had prepared herself to receive merchants from Nubia. She was taken unawares, overwhelmed, totally defeated, and for the first time in her life, she bowed and said, "Your Majesty."

His eyes surveyed her intently, then settled on her gorgeous face, and he noticed her bemusement with a strange pleasure, as he watched the magic effusing seductively from her features. When she greeted him, he spoke to her in a voice possessed of clear tones and refined accent. "Do you know who I am?"

"Yes, Your Majesty," she said in her sweet musical voice. "It was my happy fortune to see you yesterday."

He could not look at her face enough, and he began to feel a drowsy numbness come over his senses and his mind, and he no longer paid heed to his will. "Kings have authority over people," he began suddenly. "They watch over their souls, and their belongings. That is why I have come to you, to bring back something precious that came into my possession."

The king put his hand under the sash and pulled out the

sandal. "Is this not your sandal?" he said as he handed it to her.

Her eyes followed Pharaoh's hand and watched incredulously as the sandal appeared from under the sash. "My sandal," she stammered.

The king laughed kindly, and without taking his eyes off her, said, "Yours, Rhadopis. That is your name, is it not?"

She lowered her head, and mumbled, "Yes, Your Majesty." She was nervous and did not say more. Pharaoh went on, "It is a beautiful sandal. The most wonderful thing about it is the picture engraved on the inside of its sole. I thought it a beautiful illustration until I set eyes on you, for now I have beheld true beauty, and I have learned a higher truth as well, that beauty, like fate, takes people unawares in ways of which they have never conceived."

She clasped her hands together and said, "My lord, I never dreamed that you would honor my palace with your presence. And as for the fact that you would bear my sandal . . . Lord, what can I say? I have lost my mind. Please forgive me, my lord. I forgot myself and left you standing."

She rushed over to her throne and, pointing to it, bowed respectfully, but he chose a comfortable couch and sat down upon it. "Come here, Rhadopis. Sit next to me," he said.

The courtesan approached until she stood in front of him, struggling to overcome her perturbation and surprise. He took her wrist in his hand, it was the first time he had touched her, and sat her down next to him. Her heart beat wildly. She put the sandal to one side and lowered her eyes. She forgot that she was Rhadopis, the one they all worshipped, who dallied with the hearts of men as she pleased. The shock had taken her completely unawares—the divine incarnation had shaken her to the core, as if a blazing light had suddenly been shone into her eyes, and she cowered like a virgin resisting her man for the first time. But then her awesome beauty entered the fray, unbeknownst to her, strong-hearted and supremely confident, and shed its enchanting radiance on the astonished eyes of the king, as the sun shines its silver rays on a sleeping plant, arousing it from its slumber to glisten enchantingly. Rhadopis's beauty was overpowering and irresistible, it burned whomever came near it, sowing madness in his mind and filling his breast with a desire that could never be quenched or satisfied.

There could not have been two people on that immortal night—Rhadopis stumbling in her confusion, and the king lost in her beauty—more in need of the mercy of the gods in all the world.

The king, desperate to hear her voice, asked her, "Why do you not ask how the sandal came into my hands?"

"Your presence has made me forget all matters, my lord," she said anxiously.

He smiled. "How did you lose it?"

The tenderness in his voice soothed her fears. "A falcon flew off with it while I was bathing."

The king sighed and looked up, as if he was reading the inscriptions on the ceiling, and closed his eyes to imagine the enchanting scene; Rhadopis, the water lapping against her naked body, and the falcon swooping down from the sky to carry off her sandal. She heard his breath, and felt it caress her cheek, and he looked once more at her face. "The falcon flew away with it and carried it to me," he said passionately. "What a wonderful story it is! But I wonder incredulously, I might never have set eyes on you if the gods had not sent to me this noble and generous falcon. What a tragic thought! I think deep inside that it must have been too much for the falcon that I did not know you when you were only an arm's length away from me, so he threw the sandal at me to rouse me from my indifference."

She was amazed. "Did the falcon throw the sandal into your hands, my lord?"

"Yes, Rhadopis. That is the beauty of the story."

"What a coincidence. It is like magic."

"Are you saying that it is a coincidence, Rhadopis? Then what is coincidence if not our determined fate?"

She sighed and said, "You speak truly, my lord. It is like one who knows but seems not to."

"I will announce my desire to all and sundry, that not one person of my people shall ever do harm to a falcon."

Rhadopis smiled a happy, enchanting smile that flashed in her mouth like a magic spell. The king felt a burning desire consume his heart. It was not his habit to resist an emotion and he succumbed with obvious enthusiasm, saying, "He is the only creature to whom I will be indebted for the most precious thing in my life, Rhadopis. How beautiful you are. Your loveliness renders all my dreams worthless."

She was delighted, as if she was hearing these words for the first time. She gazed at him with clear, sweet eyes, inflaming his passion, and in an almost plaintive voice he said, "It is as though a red hot whip were scourging my heart." He moved his face closer to hers and whispered, "Rhadopis, I want to be immersed in your breath."

She moved her face closer to his, lowering her eyelids, and he leaned forward until his nose touched hers. His fingertips caressed her long lashes and he stared enraptured into her dark eyes as the world receded, and stunned by love's power, a magic stupor engulfed him, until at length he became aware of her deep sighs. He sat upright and whispered into her ear, saying, "Rhadopis, sometimes I see my destiny; I fear that madness will be my watchword from this hour on."

Breathless, she rested her head in her palm, her heart thumping in her breast. They sat together an hour in silence, each happy with their own musings, while in reality, though they knew it not, each communed with their newfound soul mate. Then all of a sudden Rhadopis stood up and said, "Come, follow me, my lord, take a look at my palace."

It was a happy invitation, but it reminded him of matters he had almost forgotten, and he found himself obliged to apologize. What harm would it do to postpone the encounter awhile? The palace and its contents were his property.

"Not tonight, Rhadopis," he said regretfully.

"Why not, my lord?" she asked disappointedly.

"There are people who have been waiting for me for hours in the palace."

"Which people, my lord?"

The king laughed and said disdainfully, "I should have been meeting the prime minister now. Truly, Rhadopis, since the incident of the falcon I have been prey to hard work. I had harbored every intention of visiting your palace but found no opportunity. When I realized that this evening was about to go the same way as those that had preceded it, I cancelled an important meeting, so that I might see the owner of the golden sandal."

Rhadopis was astonished. "My lord," she mumbled. She was impressed by the recklessness that had led him to postpone one of those important meetings in which he presided over the fate of his kingdom so that he could see a woman who had only been in his thoughts for a matter of hours. She thought it a beautiful touch, most endearing and without equal among the deeds of lovers or the poetry of poets.

The king rose to his feet saying, "I am going now, Rhadopis. Alas, the royal palace stifles me. It is a prison enclosed in walls of tradition, but I pass through them like an arrow. Now I shall leave a beloved face to meet a loathsome one. Have you ever seen anything stranger than that? Until tomorrow, Rhadopis, my darling. Indeed, until forever."

Having uttered these words he departed in all his magnificent youthful madness.

Love

She looked back from the door through which he had disappeared and sighed, "He has gone." But in reality he had not gone. If truly he had gone she would not have been overcome by that strange drowsiness that put her between sleep and wakefulness, half remembering and half dreaming, while crowded images raced wildly across her imagination.

She was right to be happy, for she had reached the height of glory, ascended to the peak of sublimity, and savored wonders of greatness that no woman on earth had ever dreamed of. Pharaoh in his sacred person had visited her and she had enchanted him with her fragrant breath and he had exclaimed, before her very eyes, that a scourge of flame consumed his young heart. His passion had crowned her queen on the thrones of glory and beauty. Yes, she was right to be happy, though she had known the happiness of glory before. She inclined her head slightly and her eyes fell upon the sandal. Her heart fluttered and she moved her head closer until her lips touched the warrior engraved upon it.

She did not remain alone with her dreams for long, for Shayth came in. "My lady, do you wish to sleep here?" she inquired. Rhadopis did not reply, but picking up the sandal, rose sluggishly to her feet, and drifted slowly back to her bedchamber. Encouraged by her mistress's seeming inebriation,

Shayth said sadly, "What a shame, my lady, this beautiful hall that has known such entertainment and pleasure will be empty of revelers and lovers for the first time tonight. It is probably confused like me and asks, 'Where is the singing, where the dancing, where the love?' Such is your will, my lady."

The courtesan paid her no attention as she strode silently and peacefully up the stairs. Shayth had thought that her words would arouse the curiosity of her mistress, and she said excitedly, "How miserable and upset they were when I informed them you would not be coming. They exchanged looks of grief and deep sadness and went away reluctantly, dragging tails of despair behind them."

Rhadopis did not answer. She entered her beautiful bedchamber, hurried over to the mirror and looked at her reflection, smiling with satisfaction and joy, and said to herself, "If what has happened tonight is a miracle, then this reflection is a miracle too." She was filled with a happy ecstasy and she turned to Shayth and asked her, "Who do you think that man who came to visit me was?"

"Who was he, my lady? I had not seen him before today. He is a strange young man, but there is no doubt that he is of noble stock, handsome, imposing, and bold; he is headstrong like the wind, and vibrant, his feet tread firmly upon the ground and his voice commands great authority. If it were not for my fear I would say that he is not devoid of some . . ."

"Of some what?"

"Of some madness."

"Be careful."

"My lady. However great his wealth, surely he cannot outweigh all the lovers you chased away today."

"Be careful you do not say something you might regret when regret will serve you not."

“Do his riches surpass those of Commander Tahu or Governor Ani?” asked Shayth in astonishment.

“He is Pharaoh, you foolish woman,” said Rhadopis proudly.

The woman gazed into her mistress’s face, and her lower lip dropped, but she did not say a word.

“He is Pharaoh, Shayth, Pharaoh. Pharaoh himself and no one else. Not a word to anyone, you hear. Go now and leave me. I wish to be alone.”

She closed the door and strolled over to the window which looked out over the garden. Night had fallen and spread its wings over the world. Stars sparkled in the sky above and lanterns hung from the branches of the trees. It was an enchanting night. She tasted its beauty and felt for the first time how good it was to be alone at that time, so much sweeter than meeting with all those lovers. In the silence she listened to her inner thoughts and the whisperings of her heart. Memories flowed and her mind returned to a time long ago when frivolity had first stirred in her heart, before she was crowned the queen of men’s hearts on the throne of Biga, unconquerable mistress of the male soul. In those days she was a beautiful peasant girl, sprouting between the fresh moist leaves of the countryside like a ripe rose. He was a boatman with a mellow voice and legs bronzed by the sun. She could not remember giving herself to any man at the bidding of her heart save for him, and the riverbank of Biga witnessed a scene the earth had never before been fortunate enough to behold. He invited her on board his ship and she accepted, and the waves carried her from Biga to the far South, and from that day hence, all her ties to the countryside and its people were severed. The boatman disappeared from her life one day. She did not know if he had strayed or ran away or died, and she found herself all alone. But then she was not alone, for she had her beauty, and she was not cast out onto the street. A middle-aged man with a long beard and a soft heart took her in. She led a good life and she was deeply touched by his death. Then her light began to glow and caught men's eyes and they were drawn to her like moths obsessed. They threw their young hearts under her dainty feet and countless riches, and they swore allegiance to her, installing her in the palace at Biga to rule over men's hearts. And lo, she was Rhadopis. Oh, what memories!

How had her heart died after that? Was it sadness that had killed it? Or vanity, or glory? She listened to talk of love with a deaf ear and a closed heart. The most a man so passionately in love with her as Tahu could hope for was that she would offer him her cold body.

She surrendered to her memories for a long time, as if she had summoned them to bind her with the most wonderful days of her life and the happiest. Time passed without her knowing if it was hours or minutes, until at length she heard the sound of footsteps. Annoyed she turned round and saw the door open. Shayth entered out of breath and said, "My lady, he is following me. Here he is."

She saw him enter, confidently, as if he were entering his own bedchamber. She was astonished, and overjoyed. "My lord," she exclaimed.

Shayth withdrew and closed the door. The king cast a glance around the beautiful chamber and laughed, "Should I ask forgiveness for bursting in like this?"

She smiled happily. "The chamber and its mistress are yours, my lord."

He laughed his charming laugh. It was a youthful wholesome laugh, bursting with life. He took hold of her elbow and led her over to the couch, and sitting her down, he took his seat next to her. "I feared that you might fall asleep before I came," he said.

"Asleep. Sleep would never find his way into a night like this. The light of joy would make him think it daytime."

His face turned serious. "How much more so if we should shine together."

She had never felt such happiness before, her heart had never been so awake, so alive, and she had never known the pleasure of surrender as she knew it now before this remarkable human being. He was right. She was burning, but she did not say anything. She simply raised her eyes, overflowing with joy and brimming with love, and gazed at him. Then she spoke: "I never thought you would return this night."

"Nor did I. But the meeting was heavy and tiresome, and I grew weary with concentrating. I felt troubled and restless. The man placed many decrees in front of me and I signed a few of them and listened to him with my mind distracted, until I could take no more and told him to put off the work until tomorrow. I did not think to return, I wanted to be alone that I might confer with myself. But once alone I found the solitude weighed down on me, and the night grew dreary and unbearable. Thereupon I scolded myself and said, 'Why should I wait until tomorrow?' It is my habit not to resist an emotion, so I did not hesitate, and here I am, with you."

What a happy habit it was, and she was reaping its most delicious fruits. She felt by his side a wonderful joy as he trembled with life and passion. "Rhadopis, what a beautiful name that is. It falls upon my ears like music and means 'love' in my heart. This love is something wondrous. It can disarm a man whose nights are filled with gorgeous women of every color and taste. It is truly remarkable. I wonder how it works. It seems to be a feeling of unease that torments my heart, at once a divine incantation recited on the loftiest plane of my soul, and yet a painful longing. It is you. Your stunning presence abides in every manifestation of the world and the soul. Look at this strong frame of mine, it feels a need for you as a drowning man feels the need for air to breathe."

She shared his feelings and sensed his sincerity. He had spoken to describe one heart and had described two. Like him, she could hear the divine incantation, and beheld his image in the manifestations of the world and the soul, while her eyelids were heavy with dreams and ecstasy. At last their eyelashes touched and he asked her gently, "Why do you not speak, Rhadopis?"

She opened her beautiful eyes and looked at him with passion and longing. "What need have I of words, my lord? For so long, words flowed from my tongue and my heart was dead. But now, my heart is bursting with life and soaks up your words like the earth soaks up the warmth of the sun, and through it finds life."

He smiled at her happily. "This love has plucked me from amidst a world replete with women."

She returned his smile. "And it has plucked me from amidst a world overflowing with men."

"I was stumbling about in my world, confused, and you were only an arm's length away from me. What a pity. I should have met you years ago."

"We were both waiting for the falcon to bring us together."

He held her hand tighter in his. "Yes, Rhadopis, the Fates were waiting for the falcon to appear on our horizon that they might set down on its page the most beautiful love story. I do not doubt that the falcon could not bear to put off our love any longer. We should not be apart after today.

The most beautiful thing in the world is that we should be together."

She sighed from the depths of her heart, "Yes, my lord, we should never be apart after this day. Here is my bosom for you, a verdant pasture for you to graze upon whenever you wish."

He opened her palm between his hands and he squeezed it affectionately. "Come to me, Rhadopis. Let this palace be closed and its unclean past be forgotten, for I feel that every day that was wasted of my life before I knew you is a treacherous blow directed at my happiness."

She had felt like one intoxicated, but now worrying doubts assailed her and she asked, "Does His Majesty wish me to move to his harem?"

He nodded his head, "You shall reside in its finest quarters."

She lowered her eyes, dumbfounded, not knowing what to say. Her silence took him aback and he placed the fingers of his right hand under her delicate chin and lifted her face toward him. "What is the matter?"

She hesitated a moment then asked him, "Is that an order Your Majesty?"

A look of dejection crossed his face when he heard the words "an order." He said, "Of course not, Rhadopis. The language of orders has no place in love. I would never have wished before today to be stripped of my station and become again a human being making his way in life without assistance, encountering his fortune without favor. Forget Pharaoh for a moment and tell me if you do not want to spend your life with me."

She was afraid he might misunderstand her concern and hesitation, and she said sincerely, "My desire for you, my lord, is as my desire for life itself. But the truth is more beautiful than that. The truth is that I have never truly loved life until I loved you. And the value of life for me now is that it makes me feel your love, and all my senses rejoice at your presence. Is it not an instinctive quality of lovers that they speak the truth? Ask the heart of Rhadopis, Your Majesty, and you will hear what I have already said. But I am confused and must ask why should I close the doors of my palace forever? It is me myself, Your Majesty, and you should love it as you love me. There is not a single part of it that I have not touched, my picture, my name, a statue of me. How can I ever leave it, for here descended the falcon that flew to you with the immortal message of love? How can I ever leave it when here love stirred in my heart for the first time? How can I ever leave it, my lord, when you yourself visited me here? It is worthy of any place where your feet have tread to belong, as my heart does, to you alone, and to never close its doors, ever."

He listened to her, his senses sharpened, his heart burning and irrepressible. His soul concurred with every word she spoke, and stroking the tresses of her jet-black hair, he took her in his arms and planted upon her lips a kiss moist with sweet nectar.

"Rhadopis," he said, "O love that has blended with my soul, the doors of this palace will not be closed, its rooms will not be plunged into darkness. It will remain, as we have become, a cradle for love, an amorous paradise, a lush garden wherein the seeds of memories are sown. I shall make of it a monument to love and I will cover its floor and walls with pure gold."

Her face glowed with happiness, as she confided in him, "May your will be done, Your Majesty. I swear by my love for you that tomorrow I shall go to the temple of Sothis and wash my body with sacred oil to cleanse myself of this wicked past, and I shall return to the sanctuary with a pure new heart, like a flower pierces its sheath and turns its face to the rays of the sun."

He put her hand on his heart and looked into her eyes, saying, "Rhadopis, today I am happy, I bear witness before the universe and the gods of my happiness. This is how I want my life to be. Look at me. Your dark eyes are more delicious to me than all the light of the world."

That night the island of Biga slept while love lodged for the first time in its white palace, until the coal-black night gave way before the dreamy blueness of the dawn.

The Shadow of Love

It was late morning when she awoke. The air was hot and the blazing rays of the sun sent light and fire into the world. Her fine nightshift clung to her lissome body and her hair was spread about in disarray, with tresses draped over her bosom and others cascading onto the pillow.

Blessed is an awakening that stirs beautiful memories in the heart. Her heart was a pasture of joy and the scent of flowers wafted in the air around her and the world smiled with happiness and joy. She felt with all her senses rejuvenated, that a radiant new world had been revealed to her, or that she had been created anew.

She rolled over on to her side and looked at the pillow: the hollow where his head had lain was clearly visible and it drew from her eyes a look of deep affection and compassion. She moved her head toward it and kissed it as she murmured happily, "How beautiful everything is, and how happy I am."

She sat up for a moment and then got out of bed—as she did every morning—energetic, cheerful, like a brilliant wisecrack in a soul bursting with good humor. She bathed in cold water and put on her perfume, then dressed in her garments that had been perfumed with incense and went to her dining table where she ate a breakfast of eggs and flat bread and drank a cup of fresh milk and a glass of beer.

She boarded her barge for Abu. Once there, she headed to the temple of Sothis and entered through its mighty portal with a timid heart and her spirit full of hope and expectation. She wandered through the vast building, taking in the blessings from the walls and columns which were adorned with sacred inscriptions. She placed a generous donation in the offering box, then paid a visit to the chamber of the high priestess and asked her to wash her with sacred oil to purify her of the stains and blemishes of life and its afflictions and to cleanse her heart of transgression and blindness. As she surrendered herself to the hands of the pure and chaste priestesses, it seemed to her that she was ruthlessly depositing into a grave of oblivion the body of Rhadopis, the flirtatious courtesan, who mocked men and wreaked havoc on their souls, and danced on the remains of her victims and the remnants of their shattered hearts. She felt new blood flow in her veins, and contentment, happiness, and purity throbbed in her heart and reached out to all her senses. Then she fell to her knees and prayed fervently, her eyes full of tears, humbly beseeching the god to bless her love and her new life. So happy was she as she returned to her palace that she felt like a bird spreading its wings in a clear sky. Shayth could hardly contain her joy when she greeted her. "Blessed be this happy day, my lady," she beamed. "Do you know who came to our palace while you were away?"

Her heart beat fast and furious. "Who?" she cried.

"Some men came," said the slave, "the finest of Egypt's craftsmen sent by Pharaoh. They looked at the rooms and corridors and halls, and measured the height of the windows and walls in order to make new furnishings."

"Really?"

"Yes, my lady. Soon this palace will be the wonder of the age. What a profitable deal it is!"

Rhadopis was not sure what the woman meant. Then it occurred to her and she knit her brow. "What deal do you mean, Shayth?" she asked.

The woman winked. "The deal of your new romance," she said. "By the gods, my lord is worth an entire nation of wealthy men. After today I will not be sorry to see the backs of the merchants of Memphis and the commanders of the South."

Rhadopis's face turned red with rage. "That is enough, woman!" she shouted. "This is no business deal."

"I am sorry. If I were brave enough, my lady, I would ask you what you were doing then."

Rhadopis sighed, "Stop your idle prattle. Can you not see that I am serious about this?"

The slave girl stared at her mistress's beautiful face and was silent for a moment, then said, "May the gods bless you my lady. I am confused, and am asking myself why my lady is serious?"

Rhadopis sighed again and threw herself down on the divan. "I am in love, Shayth," she said quietly.

The slave girl beat her chest with her hand. "You are in love, my lady!" she said alarmed and astonished.

"Yes, I am in love. Why are you so surprised?"

"I beg your pardon, my lady. Love is a new visitor. I have not heard you mention his name before. How did he come?"

Rhadopis smiled and said as if in a dream, "It is no cause for surprise, a woman in love. It is a common enough thing."

"Not here though," said Shayth as she pointed to her mistresses heart. "I always thought it was an impregnable fortress. How did it fall? Tell me, by God."

Dreams shone in Rhadopis's eyes, and the memory evoked exuberant feelings in her soul. "I have fallen in love, Shayth," she said in a voice that was a whisper. "And love is a wonderful thing. At what moment in time love knocked at the door of my heart, how it stole into the depths of my soul, I have no idea. It confuses me enormously, but I knew the truth in my heart, for it beat in violent turmoil, and stirred when I saw his face and when I heard his voice. I never knew it to stir at any of those things before, but a hidden voice whispered in my ear that this man and no other would own my heart. I was overcome by a violent, sweet, painful sensation, and felt an unmistakable feeling that he should be a part of me like my heart is, and I should be a part of him like his soul. I can no longer imagine how life can be good and existence pleasant without this blending of ourselves."

"How perplexing, my lady," said Shayth breathlessly.

"Yes, Shayth. As long as I enjoyed total freedom, I took up my seat atop a high hill and my eyes roamed over a strange wide world. I would spend the evening with dozens of men, enjoying pleasant conversation, delighting in works of art, savoring lewd jokes and bawdiness, and singing, yet all the time an inconsolable weariness weighed down on my heart, and an unbearable loneliness lay over my soul. Now, Shayth, my hopes are narrowed down and concentrated on one man—my lord. He is my whole world. Life has stirred again and chased away the weariness and loneliness that lay in my path and shone forth light and bliss upon it. I lost my self in this wide world and now I have found it again in my beloved. See what love can do, Shayth!"

The slave nodded her head in bewilderment and said, "It is a wonderful thing as you say, my lady. Perhaps it is sweeter than life itself. Indeed, I ask myself what I myself feel of love. Love is like hunger and men are like food. I love men as much as I love food. I don't worry about it, and that is enough for me."

Rhadopis laughed a delicate laugh like a note plucked on a harp string, and rising to her feet, went to the balcony that looked over the garden. She ordered Shayth to bring her the lyre, for she felt a desire to play the strings and sing. Why not, when the whole world was joined in joyful serenade?

Shayth disappeared for a moment then returned carrying the lyre and placed it before her mistress. "Would it bother you to delay the music for a while?" she said.

"Why?" asked Rhadopis as she picked up the lyre.

"One of the slaves asked me to inform you that there is someone who seeks permission to meet you."

A look of disapproval crossed her face. "Does he not know who it is?" she asked curtly.

"He says he is . . . he claims he has been sent by the artist Henfer."

She recalled what Henfer had said to her two days previously about the pupil he had appointed to take his place in carrying out the decoration of the summer room. "Bring him to me," she told Shayth.

She felt irritated and annoyed. She held tightly onto the lyre and her fingertips plucked the strings softly, then angrily, playing music with no unity between its parts.

Shayth returned followed by a young man, who bowed his head in reverence and said in a soft voice, "May the gods make happy your day, my lady."

She put the lyre to one side and looked at him through her long eyelashes. He was of average height, slender build, and dark complexion with handsome features and remarkably wide eyes in which appeared signs of candor and naïveté. She was taken by his young age and the sincerity in his eyes, and she wondered if he would really be able to complete the work of the great sculptor Henfer. But she was pleased to see him and the wave of irritation that had come over her moments before disappeared. "Are you the pupil whom the sculptor Henfer has chosen to decorate the summer room?" she asked him.

"Yes, my lady," said the youth with obvious embarrassment as his eyes wavered between the face of Rhadopis and the balcony floor.

"Excellent. What is your name?"

"Benamun, Benamun Ben Besar."

"Benamun. And how old are you Benamun? You look young to me."

He blushed, and said, "I will be eighteen next Misra."

"I think you may be exaggerating a little."

"Certainly not, my lady. I am telling the truth."

"What a child you are, Benamun."

A look of unease appeared in his wide, honey-colored eyes, as if he were afraid that she would object to him because of his young age. She read his fears and smiled, saying, "Do not worry. I know that a sculptor's gift is in his hands, not in his age."

"My master, the great artist Henfer, has borne witness to my ability," he said enthusiastically.

"Have you carried out important work before?"

"Yes, my lady. I decorated one side of the summer room in the palace of Lord Ani, governor of Biga."

"You are a child prodigy, Benamun."

He blushed and his eyes flashed with delight. He was overjoyed. Rhadopis summoned Shayth and ordered her to take him to the summer room. The youth hesitated a moment before following the slave and said, "You should be free for me every day, at any time you wish."

"I am used to such duties. Will you carve a full image of me?"

"Or half. Or maybe I will just do the face. It will depend on the general design of the work."

He bowed and followed Shayth out of the room. Rhadopis remembered sculptor Henfer and considered the irony: had it occurred to him that the palace he had asked her to open to his pupil would now be forbidden to him forever?

She felt relief at the effect this naïve young man had left in her, for he seemed to have provoked in her heart a new emotion that had not come to life before. It was the maternal instinct, for how quickly compassion for him had glowed in her eyes, from whose magic no man had found salvation. She prayed sincerely to Sothis to preserve his trusting candor and to deliver him from pain and despair.

Benamun

The next morning, as she had promised, she went to the summer room in the garden. There she found Benamun sitting at a table. He had spread out a sheet of papyrus upon it and was drawing shapes and images, deeply engrossed in his work. When he became aware of her presence he set down his pen, rose to his feet, and bowed to her. She greeted him and, smiling, said, "I shall make this hour of the morning for you, for it is the one I possess in my long day."

"Thank you, my lady," said the boy in his shy quiet voice. "But we shall not begin today. I am still working on the general idea of the design."

"Alas, you have deceived me, young man."

"God forbid, my lady. But I have had a wonderful idea."

She looked at his wide clear eyes and with a hint of mockery in her voice said, "You mean that young head of yours can come up with wonderful ideas?"

His face went red, and he pointed to the right wall in embarrassment and said, "I will fill that space with a picture of your face and neck."

"How awful. I fear it might turn out frightful and ugly."

"It will be beautiful as it is now."

The youth spoke these words with a simple innocence, and she looked at him intently. He was quickly embarrassed and she felt sorry for him and looked straight ahead so that her eyes settled upon the pool beyond the eastern door of the room. What a delicate young man he was, like an innocent virgin. He caused a strange compassion to stir in her heart and awakened the sleeping mother in the deep recesses of her soul. She turned to him and found him bent over his work, but he was not entirely absorbed in it, for the redness of embarrassment still shone on his cheeks. Should she not leave him and go on her way? But she felt a desire to talk to him, which she gave in to. "Are you from the South?" she asked.

The youth raised his head, his face clothed in a cheerful, happy light and answered, "I am from Ambus, my lady."

"You are from the north of the South then. So what brought you together with sculptor Henfer, since he is from Bilaq?"

"My father was a friend of sculptor Henfer, and when he saw my keen interest in art he sent me to him and commended me to his charge."

"Is your father an artist?"

The youth was silent for a moment, then said, "Not at all. My father was the senior physician of Ambus. He was a distinguished chemist and embalmer. He made numerous discoveries in methods of mummification and the composition of poisons."

Rhadopis concluded from the way he was speaking that his father was dead. But she was impressed by his discovery of the composition of poisons and asked, "Why did he manufacture poisons?"

"He used them as beneficial medicines," replied the boy sadly. "Physicians used to take them from him, but sadly, it cost him his life in the end."

"How was that, Benamun?" she asked him with great concern.

"I recall, my lady, that my father concocted a wonderful poison. He always used to boast that it was the deadliest of all poisons and could finish off its victim in a matter of seconds. For that reason he called it the 'happy poison.' Then one sad night he spent the entire night in his laboratory working ceaselessly. In the morning he was found stretched out on his bench, the spirit gone out of him, and by his side was a phial of the deadly poison, its seal broken open."

"How strange! Did he commit suicide?"

"It is certain that he took a dose of the deadly poison, but what was it that drove him to perdition? His secret was buried with him. We all believed that some devilish spirit had possessed him and caused him to lose all reason and he carried out his deed in a state of incapacity and confusion. Our entire family was devastated."

A deep sadness covered his face and he lowered his head over his chest. Rhadopis regretted she had brought up this painful subject and asked, "Is your mother still alive?"

"Yes, my lady. She still lives in our palace in Ambus. As for my father's laboratory, no one has entered its door since that night."

Rhadopis returned to her chambers thinking of the strange death of the physician Besar and his poisons locked up in the closed laboratory.

Benamun was the only outsider to appear on the calm horizon of her world of love and tranquility, as indeed he was the only person to snatch an hour from the time she allotted to love every morning. Despite this, he did not annoy her in the slightest for he was lighter and more delicate than a sprite. The days passed with her madly in love and him bent over his work, while the sublime spirit of art breathed its life into the walls of the summer room.

She delighted in watching his hand as it diffused the spirit of wondrous beauty through the room. She became convinced of his outstanding talents and felt certain that he would be ready to take over from sculptor Henfer before very long. One day she asked him, as she was about to leave the room after an hour's sitting, "Do you never feel tired or bored?"

The young man smiled proudly and said, "Not at all."

"It is as if you are driven by some demonic power."

A brilliant smile flashed across his dark face and he said quietly, naïvely, "It is the power of love."

Her heart fluttered at these words that awoke in her delicious associations conjuring up in her mind a beloved image surrounded by splendor and radiance, yet he did not comprehend a thing that went on in her soul.

"Do you not know, my lady, that art is love?" he went on.

"Really?"

He pointed to the top of her forehead, which he had drawn on the wall, and said, "Here is my soul pure and unsullied."

She had regained control of her emotions and said sarcastically, "But it is just deaf stone."

"It was stone before my hands touched it, but now I have put myself into it."

She laughed. "You are so in love with yourself!" she said as she turned her back on him; but it was clear after that day that his self was not the only thing he loved. She was walking aimlessly in the garden one day like a lost thought in a happy dreaming head, when she looked out suddenly over the summer room. She felt an urge to amuse herself by climbing the high hill in the sycamore glade and looking through the window of the room where she could see the picture of her face nearing completion directly in front of her on the opposite wall. She saw the young artist at the bottom of the wall and thought at first that he was absorbed in his work, as was his wont. Then she saw him kneel down, his arms folded across his chest, his head raised as if he was deep in prayer, except that his head was turned toward the head and face of her that he had engraved.

Her instinct drove her to hide behind a bough and she continued to watch him furtively with surprise and some alarm. She saw him rise to his feet as if he had finished his prayer, and wipe his eyes with the edge of his wide sleeve. Her heart quivered, and she remained for a moment motionless, surrounded by absolute silence. All she could hear was the intermittent cries of the ducks and their flapping as they swam on the water, then she turned round and raced back down to the palace.

What she had hoped would not happen, out of compassion for him, had happened. She had observed its possibility in his honest eyes every time he stared at her, but she had been unable to avert the calamity. Should she keep him far away from her? Should she close the door of the palace in his face with any pretext she could think to use against him? But she was concerned she might torment his delicate soul. She did not know what to do.

Her dilemma did not last long however. Nothing in the universe was capable of taking possession of her consciousness for more than a fleeting moment, for all her feelings and emotions were the booty of love, possessions in the hands of a covetous and eager lover whose desire for her knew no bounds. He would fly to her palace of dreams, renouncing his own palace and his world, unhindered by regret. Together they would escape existence, seeking refuge in their own love-filled spirits, succumbing to the magic and allure of their passion, consumed by its fire, seeing the rooms and the garden and the birds through its wonder and grandeur.

The greatest cause for concern that Rhadopis felt those days was that she might discover, in the morning after he had bade her farewell, that she had omitted to ask him whether it was her eyes that stirred his desire or her lips. As for Pharaoh, he might remember on his way back to his palace that he had not kissed her right leg as affectionately as he had her left, and perhaps this regret would cause him to rush back to erase from his mind this most trivial cause for concern.

They were days unlike any other.

Khnumhotep

The times that had granted happiness and joy to some brought sullen gloom to the face of the prime minister and high priest, Khnumhotep. The man sat in the government house observing events with a pessimistic eye, listening to what was said with keen ears and a sad heart. Then he resorted to patience, as much as patience allowed.

The decree issued by the king to sequester the temple estates had caused him untold anguish, and had placed a number of psychological crises in the way of effective government, for the mass of the priests had received the announcement with alarm and pain, and most of them had been quick to write petitions and solicitations and send them to the prime minister and lord chamberlain.

Khnumhotep had noticed that the king had not been granting him a tenth of the time he had granted him before, and it was now rare that he managed to meet him and discuss with him the affairs of the kingdom at all. It was widely rumored that Pharaoh had fallen in love with the courtesan of the white palace of Biga and that he spent his nights there with her. Moreover, groups of craftsmen had been seen driving to her palace together with gangs of slaves carrying sumptuous furniture and precious jewels. Senior figures were whispering that the palace of Rhadopis was being turned into an abode of gold, silver, and pearl, and that its columns were witness to a steamy love affair that was costing Egypt a fortune.

Khnumhotep had a wise old head on his shoulders and was possessed of keen insight, but his patience was running thin and he could remain impassive no longer. He thought long and deep about the matter and determined he would do his utmost to divert events from the direction in which they were heading. He sent a messenger to Lord Chamberlain Sofkhatep requesting the pleasure of his company at the government house. The lord chamberlain hurried over to meet him. The prime minister shook his hand and said, "I thank you, venerable Sofkhatep, for accepting my request."

The lord chamberlain bowed his head and said, "I do not hesitate to carry out my sacred duty in serving my lord."

The two men sat down facing one another. Khnumhotep had an iron will and nerves of steel and his face remained placid despite the troubling thoughts that raged in his breast. He listened to the words of the lord chamberlain in silence then said, "Venerable Sofkhatep, all of us serve Pharaoh and Egypt with loyalty."

"That is correct, Your Excellency."

Khnumhotep decided to bring up his grave business in hand and said, "But my conscience is not happy with the way events are moving these days. I am encountering problems and inconveniences. I am of the opinion, and I think that I am telling the truth, that a meeting between you and me would undoubtedly be of great benefit."

"It gives me great pleasure, by the gods, that your intuition is correct, Your Excellency."

The prime minister nodded his large head in an indication of approval, and when he spoke his tone displayed wisdom.

"It is better that we be open, for openness, as our philosopher Kagemni has pointed out, is a sign of honesty and sincerity."

Sofkhatep agreed. "Our philosopher Kagemni spoke the truth."

Khnumhotep spent a moment gathering his thoughts and then spoke with a hint of sadness in his voice. "It is very rare that I have the opportunity to meet His Majesty these days."

The prime minister waited for Sofkhatep to comment, but he remained silent, and Khnumhotep continued, "And you know, venerable sir, that many times I request an appointment to meet him, and I am informed that His Worshipful Self is out of the palace."

"It is not for any person to ask Pharaoh to account for his comings and goings," replied Sofkhatep without hesitation.

"That is not what I mean," said the prime minister. "But I believe it is my right as prime minister to be accorded the opportunity to stand before His Majesty from time to time, in order to carry out my duties as efficiently as possible."

"I beg your pardon, Your Excellency, but you do gain audiences with Pharaoh."

"Very rarely does the opportunity present itself, and you will find that I do not know what I should do to present to His Sublime Self the petitions that are overflowing the government offices."

The lord chamberlain scrutinized him for a moment and then said, "Perhaps they are to do with the temple estates?"

A sudden light sparkled in the prime minister's eye. "That is it, sir."

"Pharaoh does not wish to hear anything new about the subject," said Sofkhatep quickly, "for he has spoken his final word on the matter."

"Politics does not know final words."

"That is your opinion, Your Excellency," said Sofkhatep sharply, "and it could be that I do not share it with you."

"Are not the temple estates a traditional inheritance?"

Sofkhatep disapproved, for he sensed that the prime minister was trying to draw him into a conversation that he did not wish to partake in. Indeed, he had already made his reluctance quite clear, and in a tone that left no room for doubt, he said, "I am happy to take His Majesty's word at face value, and I will go no further."

"The most loyal of His Majesty's subjects are those who give him sound and sincere advice."

The lord chamberlain was most indignant at the abrasiveness of these words, but he suppressed the rage at his offended pride, saying, "I know my duty, Your Excellency, but I do not question it except before my conscience."

Khnumhotep sighed in despair, and then said with quiet resignation, "Your conscience is beyond all suspicion, venerable sir, and I have never been in any doubt about your loyalty or your wisdom. Perhaps that is what led me to seek your guidance on the matter. As for the fact that you believe that this does not agree with your loyalty, then I regret that I will have to do without you. Now I have only one request."

"And what is that, Your Excellency?" said Sofkhatep.

"I would request that you bring it to the attention of Her Majesty the Queen that I seek the honor of meeting her today."

Sofkhatep was taken aback, and stared at the prime minister in amazement, for even if the man had not overstepped the mark with this request, it was certainly unexpected, and the lord chamberlain was perplexed.

"I am presenting this request in my capacity as the prime minister of the kingdom of Egypt," he said firmly.

Sofkhatep was worried. "Shall I not wait until tomorrow so that I may inform the king of your desire?"

"Indeed not, venerable sir. I am requesting the assistance of Her Majesty the Queen in order to surmount the obstacles which stand in my way. It is a golden opportunity that cannot be missed for me to serve my king and my country."

There was nothing Sofkhatep could do except to say, "I will put your request to Her Majesty at once."

"I shall await your messenger," said Khnumhotep as he shook Sofkhatep's hand.

"As you wish, Your Excellency," said the lord chamberlain.

Once alone, Khnumhotep frowned and gritted his teeth so tightly that his wide chin looked like a slab of granite as he paced up and down the room deep in thought. He did not doubt the loyalty of Sofkhatep, but he had little faith in his courage and determination. He had called on him because he had not wanted to leave any stone unturned, but he had had little hope in the outcome. He wondered with some disquiet if the queen would accept his request and invite him to meet her. What on earth would he do if she refused? The queen was not to be dismissed lightly. Perhaps with her keen intelligence she would be able to unravel this complex knot and rescue the relationship between the king and the clergy from collapse and disintegration. No doubt the queen was aware of the young king's misbehavior, and was seriously pained by it, for she was a queen well known for her astute mind, and she was a wife who felt joy and sadness like other wives. Was it not regrettable that the properties of the temples were being stripped, wrested away from them so that their yields might be squandered under the feet of a dancer?

Gold was pouring into the palace at Biga through the doors and windows. The finest craftsmen in the land were flocking there and working day and night to make furniture for its rooms, jewelry for its mistress, and adornments for her clothes. And where . . . where was Pharaoh? He had abandoned his wife, his harem, and his ministers, and wanted no more from the world than to spend his time in the palace of that bewitching harlot.

The man sighed a deep sad sigh and muttered to himself, "He who sits on the throne of Egypt should not spend his time in dalliance."

He was soon lost in deep thought, but he did not wait long, for his chamberlain entered and asked permission for a messenger from the palace to see him. The prime minister granted him leave to enter and waited for the man with bated breath, for despite his strong will and nerves of steel his lips were twitching at that decisive moment. The messenger came in and bowed his head in greeting. "Her Majesty the Queen is waiting for Your Excellency," he said tersely.

He immediately gathered up the bundle of petitions and went to his chariot which sped him to the palace. He never imagined that the messenger would come so quickly. The queen was clearly troubled and sad, suffering from the pangs of her lonely isolation. No doubt she was struggling to maintain her composure under the strain of insult and deprivation, brooding behind an unbending façade of silence and pride. He sensed that she was of his opinion and that she saw events as the clergy, and indeed all intelligent citizens, saw them. In any case, he would do his duty and let the gods decree what should come to pass.

He reached the palace and went straight to the queen's chambers. He was soon invited to meet Her Majesty in the official reception hall. He was ushered into the hall and headed toward the throne. Bowing his head until his forehead touched the hem of the queen's garment, he said with great solemnity, "Peace be upon Your Majesty, Light of the Sun, Splendor of the Moon."

"Peace be upon you, Prime Minister Khnumhotep," said the queen softly.

The prime minister resumed an erect posture, though his head remained lowered. "The tongue of your most obedient slave is unable to express its thanks to Your Sublime Being for your kindness in granting him this audience," he said humbly.

The queen spoke in her measured tone, "I believe that you would not request an audience except for the most urgent of matters. For that reason I did not hesitate to receive you."

"May Your Majesty's wisdom be exalted, for the matter is indeed most grave, concerning as it does the very essence of national policy."

The queen waited silently while the man mustered his strength. Then he continued, "Your Majesty, I am colliding with strong obstacles such that I have come to fear that I am not able to carry out my duty in a way that pleases both my conscience and His Majesty, Pharaoh."

He was silent for a moment and snatched a quick look at the queen's calm face as if to examine the effect his words had had on her, or to await a word of encouragement for him to elaborate. The queen understood the meaning of his hesitation and said, "Speak, Prime Minister, I am listening to you."

"I am colliding with these obstacles," he said, "as a result of the decree issued by the king to seize most of the temple properties. The priests are troubled and have resorted to petitions which they have obediently submitted to Pharaoh, for they know that the temple estates were granted by the pharaohs favorably and in good faith. They are concerned that the revoking of the privilege will be greatly resented."

The prime minister was silent for a moment then continued, "The clergy, Your Majesty, are the king's soldiery in time of peace. Peace needs men of sterner mettle than men of war, and among them are teachers, physicians, and preachers, while others are ministers and governors. They would not hesitate to give up their properties gladly if the harshness of war or famine required them to do so, but . . ." The man hesitated for a moment, then, lowering his voice, he continued, "But what saddens them is to see this wealth spent in other ways. . . ."

He did not want to overstep this careful limit of allusion, for he had no doubt that she understood everything and knew everything. But she did not comment on his words, and seeing no alternative but to present to her the petitions, he said, "These petitions, Your Majesty, express the feelings of the high priests of the temples. My lord, the king, has refused to look at them. Could my lady peruse them, for the complainants are a portion of your loyal people and deserve your consideration."

The queen accepted the petitions, and the prime minister placed them on a large table and stood silently, his head lowered. The queen made no promises, nor had he expected her to, but he was optimistic that the petitions had been received. Then she gave him permission to depart and he withdrew with his hands over his eyes.

On his way back, the prime minister said to himself, "The queen is extremely sad. Perhaps her sadness will serve our just cause."

Nitocris

The prime minister disappeared through the door and the queen was left alone in the large hall. She leaned her crowned head against the back of the throne, closed her eyes, and sighed deeply. The breath came out hot and stifled with sadness and pain. How long she had been patient and how much she had suffered. Not even those nearest to her knew of the tongues of flame that scorched her innards without mercy, for she had continued to regard people with a face like the Sphinx, calm and shrouded in silence.

There was nothing about the matter that she did not know. She had witnessed the tragedy from the first scene. She had seen the king topple into the abyss, fall prey to an untamable passion, and rush into the arms of that woman, whose ravishing beauty every tongue extolled, without a thought for anyone else. A poisoned arrow had pierced her self-respect and wound its way into her deepest, inmost emotions. But she had not flinched, and a violent struggle had arisen in her breast between the woman with a heart and the queen with a crown. The experience had proven that like her father, she was unyielding; the crown had tempered the heart and pride had smothered love. She had withdrawn within her sad self, a prisoner behind curtains, and so she had lost the battle and emerged from it broken winged, not having fired a single arrow from her bow.

The real irony was that they were still newly wed, though that short time had been sufficient to reveal the violent defiance and capricious passion that his soul harbored, for he had wasted no time in filling the harem with countless slave girls and concubines from Egypt, Nubia, and the lands of the North. She had paid no attention to them, for none of them had driven him away from her and she had continued to be his queen, and the queen of his heart, until that enchanting woman had appeared on his horizon and so fatally attracted him, altogether taking over his emotions and his mind, and totally distracting him from his wife, his harem, and his loyal advisers. Hope had played with her deceptively for a time and then given her over to despair, despair shrouded in pride, and she felt her heart imbibing the agony of death.

There were times when madness coursed through her veins and a fleeting light shone in her eyes. She wanted to jump up and thrash about and avenge her broken heart, then quickly she would say to herself with great scorn, "How can it be right for Nitocris to compete with a woman who sells her body for pieces of gold?" Her blood would cool down and the sadness would freeze in her heart like deadly poison in the stomach.

But today it had been proven to her that there were hearts other than hers suffering pain as a result of the king's irresponsibility. Here was Khnumhotep complaining to her of his concerns, and telling her quite openly, "It is not right that the property of the temples should be seized so that Rhadopis the dancer can squander it." Moreover, the cream of the wise men believed in what he was saying. Should she not come out of her silence? If she did not speak now, then when was she supposed to cure his madness with her wisdom? It pained her that these whispered grumblings should reach the unshakeable throne. She felt that her duty required her to remove the apprehensions and to restore some semblance of order. What did her pride matter? She would step on it. She resolved to move forward with steadfast steps along the path of equanimity, with the help of the gods.

The queen was relieved with this line of thought that had come about as a result of her wisdom and inner conviction. Her former stubbornness disappeared, having persevered long and desperately, and now she was firmly resolved to confront the king with strength and sincerity.

She left the hall and returned to her royal chamber, and spent the remainder of the day in thought and contemplation. During the night her sleep was intermittent and fraught with torment, and she was desperate for noon to come, for that was when the king awoke after his busy night. Feeling no compunction, she walked confidently over to the king's quarters. Her unusual journey caused some commotion among the guards, and they saluted her.

"Where is His Majesty the King?" she asked one of them.

"In his private quarters, Your Majesty," replied the man reverently.

She walked slowly to the room where the king spent time on his own, and passing through the large door, she found him sitting in the center of the room a good forty feet from the entrance. The chamber was filled with works of art and opulence of indescribable beauty. The king was not expecting to see her and it had been several days since they had last met. He rose to his feet in surprise and greeted her with a nervous smile, and motioned to her to sit down. "May the gods bring you happiness, Nitocris. If I had known you wanted to see me I would have come to you," he said.

The queen sat silently and said to herself, "How does he know I did not want to meet him all this time?" then she directed her words to him. "I do not want to disturb you, Brother. I have no objection coming to you so long as it is duty which moves me."

The king paid no attention to her words because he was feeling acutely distressed, for her coming and her expressionless face had moved him. "I am embarrassed, Nitocris," he said.

She was surprised that he should say so. It had irked her slightly to see him so happy and in such good health, like a radiant flower, and despite her self-composure she was agitated. "Nothing hurts me more than your being embarrassed."

It was the most delicate insinuation but it irritated him and changed his mood. He bit his lip and said, "Sister, men are subject to oppressive desires, and may fall prey to one of them."

His admission struck cruelly at her pride and feelings, and she forgot about being reasonable and spoke honestly, "By the gods, it saddens me that you, Pharaoh, should complain of oppressive desires."

The irascible king felt the sting of her words and was roused to anger. The blood rushed to his head, and he shot to his feet, his face boding evil. The queen was afraid that his anger at her would spoil the anger on behalf of which she had come, and she regretted what she had said. "It is you who drives me to say such things, Brother," she said hopefully, "but that is not why I have come. Your anger no doubt will wax doubly when I tell you that I have come to you to discuss grave matters which touch upon the politics of the kingdom upon whose throne we sit together."

He suppressed his rage and asked her in a quieter voice, "What is it you wish to speak about, Queen?"

The queen regretted that the tone of the conversation had not set a suitable atmosphere for her purpose, but she saw no way out. "The temple estates," she said without further ado.

The king scowled. "Did you say the temple estates?" he yelled angrily. "I call them the priests' estates."

"May your will be done, Your Majesty. Changing the name changes nothing of the matter."

"Do you not know that I hate to have that phrase repeated to me?"

"I am trying to do what others cannot. My intentions are good."

The king shrugged his shoulders angrily. "And what is it you wish to say, my queen?" he asked.

"Khnumhotep requested to see me and I granted him an audience, I listened. . . ."

He did not let her finish. "Is that what the man did?" he said irately.

The queen was dismayed. "Yes. Do you find anything in his behavior that deserves your wrath?"

"I certainly do," roared the king. "He is a stubborn man. He refuses to do my bidding. I know he is loath to implement the decree. He is watching me, seeking to waylay me in the hope that he will succeed in revoking it by asking sometimes, though I have refused to listen to him, or by encouraging the priests to submit petitions, just as he urged them before to shout out his vile name. The crafty scheming prime minister is rushing blindly down the road of my enemies."

She was appalled by his thinking and said, "You do the man an injustice. I believe him to be one of the throne's most loyal servants. He is exceedingly wise; his only intention is to forge harmony. Is it not natural that the man should be saddened at the loss of privileges that his institution acquired under the auspicious beneficence of our ancestors?"

Rage flared in the king's heart, for he could find no excuse for a person who did not comply with his orders openly or in secret, and he could not accept under any circumstance, that a person might see things differently than himself. Furiously, and in a voice full of bitter sarcasm, he said, "I see that the schemer was able to change your mind, Queen."

"I was never of the opinion that the temple properties should be seized," she said indignantly, "I do not see that it is necessary."

The king's anger resurfaced and there was violence in his words. "Does it displease you that your wealth grows?"

How can he say that when he knows so well where that money is spent?

His words provoked her buried anger and her stifled fury and she flew into a rage and her feelings took control of her. "Every thinking person would be offended to see the land of the wise seized only for their revenues to be spent on frivolous pleasures."

The king was beside himself and, gesturing threateningly with his hand, said, "Woe betide that scheming man. He would be tempted to sow discord between us."

She was hurt. "You think in your own mind that I am a gullible child," she said sadly.

"Woe betide him. He asked to meet the queen so he could talk to the woman concealed behind her royal attire."

Mortified, she cried out to him, "My lord!"

But he continued, fuelled by his demonic rage, "You came, Nitocris, driven by jealousy, not by a desire for harmony."

She felt a violent blow strike at her pride and her eyes

misted over. Her pulse rang out in her ears and her limbs trembled. For a moment she could not speak. Then she said, "King, Khnumhotep does not know anything about you that I do not know myself, and yet still he rushes to inform me. And if you think that it is jealousy that inspires me, then be under no illusion. I know, as everyone knows, that you have been throwing yourself into the arms of a dancer on the island of Biga for months. In all that time have you ever seen me come after you, or try to stop you, or plead with you? And know that he who wishes to preach to a woman will slink back in failure, all he will find before him is Queen Nitocris."

Pharaoh was incensed. "You are still spewing the burning ash of jealousy," he said.

The queen stamped her foot on the floor and stood up in exasperation. "King," she said resentfully, "It does not shame a queen that she be jealous of her husband, but it truly shames a king that he should squander the gold of his nation under the feet of a dancer, and expose his pure and unsullied throne to the malicious gossip of all and sundry."

With these words the queen departed, turning a deaf ear to his protestations.

Anger engulfed the king, and he lost his composure. He considered Khnumhotep the one responsible for all his troubles. He summoned Sofkhatep and ordered him to inform Prime Minister Khnumhotep immediately that he was waiting for him. The bewildered lord chamberlain set off to carry out his lord's order. The prime minister showed up torn between hope and despair, and was shown in to the furious king. The man pronounced the traditional greeting but Pharaoh was not listening, and interrupted him harshly, "Did I not command you, Prime Minister, never to bring up the issue of the temple estates again?"

The man was shocked by the venomous tone, which he was hearing for the first time, and he felt his hopes fading. "My lord," he said desperately, "I considered it my duty to bring to your most sublime attention the grievances of a constituency of your loyal and faithful people."

"On the contrary," said the king cruelly, "you wanted to stir up the dust between myself and the queen, so that under its cover you might achieve your aim."

The man held back his hands imploringly, he wanted to speak but he could not get out more than, "My lord, my lord . . ."

"Khnumhotep," roared the furious king, "you refuse to obey my orders, I will never trust you again after today."

The high priest was speechless, frozen to the spot. His head sank to his chest in sadness and, in a tone of surrender, he said, "My lord, by the gods, it truly saddens me to withdraw from the glorious arena of your service, and I shall return as I was before, one of your loyal and insignificant slaves."

The king felt relief after he had vented his ferocious anger, and he sent for Sofkhatep and Tahu. The two men came at once, wondering why they had been summoned. "I have finished with Khnumhotep," said the king calmly.

There was deep silence. Signs of amazement appeared on Sofkhatep's face but Tahu remained unmoved. The king looked from one to the other saying, "What is the matter, why don't you speak?"

"It is a very serious matter, my lord," said Sofkhatep.

"You think it serious, Sofkhatep? And what about you, Tahu?"

Tahu was motionless, his feelings dead, no reaction in his heart to the events, but he said, "It is a deed, Your Majesty, wrought by the inspiration of the sacred and worshipful powers."

The king smiled, as Sofkhatep considered the matter from all angles. "From today Khnumhotep will find himself much freer," the chamberlain said.

Pharaoh shrugged his shoulders in disdain. "I do not think he will expose himself to danger."

Then Pharaoh continued in another tone, "And now, who do you suggest I should appoint as his successor?"

There was a moment of silence as the two men thought.

The king smiled and said, "I choose Sofkhatep. What do you think?"

"The one you have chosen, my lord, is the strongest and most faithful," said Tahu sincerely.

As for Sofkhatep, he appeared disturbed and troubled by their words, but Pharaoh was quick to persuade him, asking, "Would you abandon your king in his hour of need?"

Sofkhatep sighed and said, "Your Majesty shall find me loyal."

The New Prime Minister

Pharaoh felt a certain reassurance at the ushering in of this new era, and his anger abated. He left the affairs of state in the hands of the man he trusted and directed his attention toward the woman who had taken over his soul and heart and senses. With her, he felt that life was good, the world was blissful, and his soul full of joy.

As for Sofkhatep, the responsibility weighed heavily on his shoulders. There was no doubt in his mind that Egypt had received his appointment with caution, disapproval, and stifled indignation. He had felt isolated from the moment he stepped inside the government house. Pharaoh was content to be in love and had turned his back on all concerns and duties, and while the provincial governors paid him public homage, in their hearts they followed the priests. The prime minister looked around him and found only Commander Tahu to help and advise him, and although the two of them differed on many matters, they had in common their love for Pharaoh and their loyalty to him. The commander accepted Sofkhatep's call and stretched out his hand to help him and shared in his isolation and his many troubles. Together they struggled to save the ship tossed about on angry waves as storm clouds gathered on the horizon. But Sofkhatep lacked the qualities of an experienced captain, for though he was loyal and possessed great integrity, and in his wisdom the truth of matters were made manifest to him, he lacked courage and decisiveness. He had seen the error from the beginning, but he had not tried to rectify it as much as he had skirted about it, making light of its consequences for fear of incurring the wrath of his lord or hurting him. So it was that matters proceeded unimpeded down the road that anger had laid for them.

Tahu's vigilant spies brought back important news, saying that Khnumhotep had moved suddenly to Memphis, the religious capital. The news caused consternation between the prime minister and the commander and they were bewildered as to why the man would take upon himself the difficult journey from the South to the North. Sofkhatep expected some mischief and did not doubt that Khnumhotep would make contact with senior members of the clergy, all of whom were furious at the dire situation that had befallen them, and at the knowledge that the wealth that had been withheld from them was being prodigally scattered at the feet of a dancing girl from Biga, for there was not one person who was ignorant of this fact now. The high priest would find among them fertile ground to sow his teachings and reiterate his complaints.

The first indications of the clergy's discontent appeared when the messengers who had been sent out to announce the news of Sofkhatep's appointment as prime minister returned with official congratulations from the provinces. The priests, however, had remained alarmingly silent, moving Tahu to say, "They are starting to threaten us."

Then letters began to pour in from all the temples bearing the signatures of all the priests from all ranks petitioning

Pharaoh to review the question of the temple estates. It was a worrying and ominous consensus and it only added to Sofkhatep's woes.

One day Sofkhatep called Tahu to the government house. The commander hurried over. The prime minister pointed to his official chair of office and sighed, "That chair almost makes me dizzy."

"Your head is too great for that chair to make it dizzy," said Tahu.

Sofkhatep sighed sadly, "They have drowned me in a flood of petitions."

"Have you shown them to Pharaoh?" asked the commander with some concern.

"No, Commander. Pharaoh does not allow a single soul to bring up the subject, and it is very rare that I am granted an audience with him. I feel confused and alone."

The two men were silent for a moment, each lost in his own thoughts. Then Sofkhatep shook his head in amazement, and said, as if addressing himself, "It is magic, no doubt about it."

Tahu looked curiously at the prime minister, then suddenly understood what the man meant. A shiver ran down his spine and his face turned pale, but he managed to control his feelings, as he had become used to doing during the recent lean period of his life, and with a simplicity that required enormous effort, he asked, "What magic do you mean, Your Excellency?"

"Rhadopis," said Sofkhatep. "Does she not work her magic on Pharaoh? Nay, by the gods, what is wrong with His Majesty is clearly magic."

Tahu's spirit shook at the mention of the word. It seemed to him that he was hearing something strange, whose magical effect touched all his senses and emotions, and almost removed the plug he had stuffed mercilessly into the mouth of his emotions. He clenched his teeth and said, "People say that love is magic, and the magicians say that magic is love."

"I have come to believe that the ravishing beauty of Rhadopis is accursed magic," said the prime minister despondently.

Tahu glared at him sternly. "You did not recite the spell that made this magic, did you?"

Sofkhatep sensed the rebuke in the commander's voice and the color drained out of his face, and he spoke quickly, as one rejecting an accusation. "She was not the first woman. . . ."

"But she was Rhadopis."

"I was concerned for His Majesty's happiness."

"And you employed magic for his sake? Alas!"

"Yes, Commander. I understand that I have made a serious mistake. But now something must be done."

"That is your duty, Your Excellency," said Tahu, the bitterness still in his voice.

"I am asking your advice."

"Loyalty reaches its full extent in true and honest counsel."

"Pharaoh will not accept that anyone broaches the subject of the clergy in his presence."

"Have you not shared your opinion with Her Majesty the Queen?"

"That is the very route that led Khnumhotep to incur the wrath of His Majesty the King."

Tahu could think of nothing to say, but Sofkhatep had an idea and, speaking softly, said, "Is there perhaps not some benefit to be gained by arranging a meeting between you and Rhadopis?"

A shiver ran down Tahu's spine once again, and his heart

thumped wildly in his breast. The emotions he was trying so hard to conceal almost exploded. "The old man doesn't know what he's saying," he thought to himself. "He thinks His Majesty is the only one bewitched."

"Why do you not meet her yourself," he said to Sofkhatep.

"I think you would be more able than me to reach an understanding with her."

"I fear that Rhadopis would not be well disposed to me," he said coolly. "She may think ill of me, and spoil my efforts on Pharaoh's behalf. I think not, Your Excellency."

Sofkhatep dreaded the thought of confronting Pharaoh with the truth.

Tahu could not stay there any longer. His nerves were in turmoil, and a violent unstoppable emotion tore at his soul. He asked the prime minister's permission to leave and departed as if in a trance, leaving Sofkhatep drowning in a deep chasm of doubt and affliction.

The Two Queens

Sofkhatep was not the only one whose head was bowed by woe.

The queen had confined herself to her chambers, brooding over the sadness buried deep inside her, the ominous pain, the despair she could voice to no one, reviewing the tragedy of her life with a broken heart, and observing the events that were unfolding in the Valley with sad eyes. She was nothing other than a woman who had lost her heart, or a queen seated uneasily upon her throne. All bonds of affection between her and the king had been broken without hope of communication as long as he remained engulfed in his passion, and as long as she took recourse to her silent pride.

It distressed her to know that the king had become so abstemious in attending to his sublime duties, for love had made him forget everything until all authority rested in the hands of Sofkhatep. She harbored no doubts about the prime minister's loyalty to the throne, but she was angry at the king's recklessness and neglect. She was determined to do something, whatever it might cost her, and she did not waiver from her aim. One day, she summoned Sofkhatep and asked him to refer to her in all matters that required the opinion of the king. Thus did she allay some of her anger, and unbeknown to her, greatly relieved the prime minister, who felt a great weight had been lifted from his frail shoulders.

Having made contact with the prime minister, she learned of the latest petitions that the priests had sent from all corners of the kingdom, and she read them with patience and care. She realized immediately that the very highest authorities in the kingdom were united in their word, and she recognized the great danger concealed behind the balanced and prudent wording. Bewildered and distressed, she asked herself what would happen if the priests learned that Pharaoh paid not the slightest attention to their requests. The priesthood was a mighty force: they held sway over the people's hearts and minds, for the populace listened to the clergy in the temples, schools, and universities, and found solace in their morals and teachings, holding them up as ideals. How would events transpire, however, if the people despaired of Pharaoh's favor and lost hope of setting right matters they saw unfolding in a manner unprecedented during all the glorious and proud ages of the eternal past?

There was no doubt that events were becoming dangerously complicated, hurtling toward discord and dissent, threatening to divide the king—slumbering and dreaming on the island of Biga—and his loyal and faithful subjects, while Sofkhatep looked on in dismay, his wisdom and loyalty of no use at all.

The queen felt that something should be done and that leaving events to take their course would bring only trouble and calamity. She would have to wipe from the calm and lovely face of Egypt the decay that was descending upon it and restore its former radiance. What was she to do? The day before, she had hoped to convince her husband of the truth, but there was no hope of going to him again today. She had still not forgotten the cruel blow he had dealt her pride. Sadly, she was determined to have nothing to do with him, and she looked for a new way by which to reach her goal. But then when she thought about her goal she was not sure what it was. Finally she told herself that the most she could hope to gain was for Pharaoh to return to the priests the estates he had seized from them. But how was that to be brought about? The king was irascible, violent, and proud. He would not step down for anyone. He had ordered the confiscation of the lands in a moment of severe anger, but now there was no doubt that things other than anger pressed him to keep the lands in his possession. Anyone who knew the palace of Biga, and the gold the king was lavishing upon it, would be under no illusion as to the expense. It had come to be called the 'golden palace of Biga,' and rightly so, such was the amount of objects and furniture crafted from pure gold it contained. If this huge hole that was swallowing up the king's money were stopped, perhaps it would be easier for him to think about returning the temple estates to the clergy. She had no desire to turn the king away from the courtesan of Biga: the idea had never occurred to her, but she wanted to put an end to his extravagance. She sighed and said to herself, "Now our aim is clear: we should find a way to convince the king to renounce his wastefulness, then we can persuade him to restore the lands to their owners. But how are we to persuade the king?" She had tried to put him out of the equation but then she found him every step of the way she considered. She had failed to convince him once already, and neither Sofkhatep nor Tahu had had better luck, for the king was governed by passion and there was no way to reach him. Then the question popped into her mind, "Who can convince the king?" A painful shiver ran down her spine, for the answer came to her immediately. It was awful and painful, but she had known it all along. It was one of the truths that brought back the pain whenever the memory returned, for the Fates had decreed that the person who controlled the king, who controlled his destiny, was her rival, the dancer of Biga, who had condemned her to be forever excluded from Pharaoh's heart. That was the bitter truth and she was loath to accept it, as a person is loath to accept truths such as death, old age, and incurable disease.

The queen was a sad woman, but she was, nevertheless, a great queen with extreme foresight. And though she could put the fact that she was a woman to the back of her mind, she could not forget it altogether, for her heart continued to dwell on her husband the king and the woman who had stolen him from her. As for the fact that she was queen, that she could never put to the back of her mind, nor neglect her duties for a single moment. She was sincerely resolved to save the throne and to maintain its exaltation beyond the reach of whispered mutterings of discontent. She wondered if she had come to this decision through a sense of duty alone, or if there were other motives. Our thoughts are always driven by considerations which revolve around those we love and those we hate, for to them we are drawn by hidden forces as a moth is drawn to the light of a lamp. She had felt at the beginning a desire to see Rhadopis, whom she had heard so much about. But what did that mean? Should she go to the woman to talk to her about the affairs of Egypt? Should Queen Nitocris go to the dancer who offers herself on the market of love, and speak to the woman in the name of her alleged love for the king, that she might deter him from his wastefulness, and return him to his duty? What a repulsive thought it was.

The queen had had enough of her seclusion, she felt pressed by her hidden emotions and her obvious duty to emerge from her silence and long imprisonment. She could be patient no longer. She had convinced herself that her duty required her to do something, to make another attempt, and she wondered in her bemusement, "Shall I really go to this woman, impress her duty upon her, and ask her to save the king from the abyss toward which he is hurtling?" The very thought threw her into long and sad confusion, and she succumbed to frenzy and delirium. But she would not be distracted from her intention, and her determination grew stronger, like the flood surging downstream which cannot be turned back, but flows ever onward, turbulent, churning, and ferocious. And at the end of this dire struggle she said, "I shall go."

The next morning she waited until the king had returned, then set off just before noon on one of the royal barges for the gilded white palace of Biga. She was touched by a mood of regret and dismay, for she had not put on royal attire and she was angry with herself for that. The barge berthed by the steps of the palace and she stepped out to be greeted by a slave. She told him that she was a visitor and wished to meet the mistress of the palace and he led her to the reception hall. The air was cold and the winter wind blew icy gusts through naked branches that looked like mummified arms. She sat down in the hall and waited alone. She felt uncomfortable, helpless. She tried to console herself by telling herself that it was right for the queen to sacrifice her pride for the sake of her sublime duty. As the waiting dragged on, she wondered uneasily if Rhadopis would leave her there awhile as she did with the men. She felt a twinge of anxiety and she regretted having been so hasty as to come to the palace of her rival.

A few minutes more passed before she heard the rustle of a garment. She raised her heavy head, and her eyes fell upon Rhadopis for the first time. There was no doubt it was Rhadopis, and Nitocris felt a burning pang of despair. Face-to-face with this devastating beauty, she forgot for a moment her troubles and the purpose of her visit. Rhadopis was taken unaware as well by the sedate beauty of the queen and her dignified demeanor.

They held out their hands to one another in greeting and Rhadopis sat down next to her imposing yet unknown guest, and finding her inclined to silence she addressed her in her musical voice, "You have alighted in your own palace."

"Thank you," replied the guest curtly in a deeply solemn voice.

Rhadopis smiled and said, "Would that our guest might permit us to know her noble personage?"

It was a natural enough question, but it irritated the queen as if she had not been expecting it, and she found herself with no alternative but to announce herself. "I am the queen," she said calmly.

She looked at Rhadopis to see what effect her revelation had, and she saw the smile recede and her eyes shine with astonishment, and her breast swell up and stiffen, like a viper when it is attacked. The queen was not as calm as she appeared, for her heart had changed when she saw her rival. She felt her blood was on fire, scorching her veins, and she was filled with hatred. They had come face-to-face like two champions prepared for mortal combat. She was overcome with a feeling of bitterness deformed with anger and resentment. For a moment the queen forgot everything, save that she was looking at the woman who had plundered her happiness, and Rhadopis forgot everything, except that she was in front of the woman who shared her lover's name and throne.

Such was the atmosphere that charged their conversation from the beginning with anger and resentment, and set it on a regrettable and violent course. Moreover, the queen was displeased with her love rival's lack of respect. "Do you not know, woman, how to greet a queen?" she demanded indignantly.

Rhadopis sat frozen to the spot, a rush of violent agitation rocked her heart, and her pent-up rage almost exploded. But she controlled her nerves, for she knew another way to extract her revenge, and drawing a smile on her lips she bowed her head as she sat—she had been sitting with her head resting on the back of the chair out of languor and contempt—and said in a tone not devoid of sarcasm, "This is indeed a momentous day, Your Majesty. My palace shall be remembered by posterity."

The queen's face glowed with anger. "I could not agree more," she said sharply. "Your palace will be remembered, but fondly on this occasion, and not as the people are wont to remember it."

Rhadopis looked at her with a derision that veiled her wrath and exasperation. "Is not that an insult to the people? Are they to think ill of a palace where their lord and majesty pastures his heart and passion?"

The queen accepted this jibe gracefully and cast a meaningful glance at the courtesan. "Queens are not like other women," she said, "occupying their hearts with love."

"Is that so, Your Majesty? I thought the queen was a woman after all else."

"That is because you have never been a queen, not for a single day," said the queen with obvious irritation.

Rhadopis's breast filled up and turned to stone. "I beg your pardon, Your Majesty, but I am a queen."

The queen glared at her curiously. "Are you indeed? And over which kingdom have you ruled?" she asked mockingly.

"Over the widest kingdom of all," she said proudly, "over Pharaoh's heart."

The queen felt painfully weak, and ashamed. She knew for certain that she had sunk down to the level of the dancer by entering with her into a fight. She had shed her raiment of glory and dignity to appear naked in the skin of a jealous woman, put on the defensive to win back her man, seizing her rival by the neck, plotting her downfall. As she looked at herself and her rival sitting next to her, arrogant and haughty, firing the arrow back into her own chest, boasting to her about her husband's love and authority, she felt queer and bewildered, and she wished it were all an unpleasant and ridiculous dream.

She suppressed her emotions completely, and burying them deep in her soul, quickly regained her natural aloofness. In place of the anger and resentment, blue blood flowed in her veins, not seeking to condemn just out of pride, and remembering the purpose of her visit, she resolved to pardon the courtesan for the way she had behaved.

She looked at Rhadopis, her face now reflecting both outer and inner calm, and said, "You did not receive your queen well, madam. Perhaps you misunderstood the purpose of my visit and became angry. Rest assured I did not come to your palace on a matter of personal business."

Rhadopis was silent and shot her a look full of trepidation.

The queen's anger and resentment had not abated but she pushed them to one side and said calmly, "I have come, my lady, on far more important business, business that concerns the glorious throne of Egypt, and the peacefulness that should characterize the relations between the one on the throne and his subjects."

Rhadopis spoke with irritation and derision, "Glorious matters indeed. And what can I do about them, my lady? I am nothing but a woman whom love delights to make its full time occupation."

The queen sighed and, disregarding Rhadopis's tone of voice, said, "You look down, I look up. I had thought you might be concerned about His Majesty's honor and happiness. If I am correct, then you should not lead him astray. He is pouring mountains of gold into your palace, and wresting from the finest of his men their lands until the people cry out in pain, and moan in complaint, and say that His Majesty withholds from us money which he squanders blindly on a woman he loves. Your duty, if you are truly concerned for his honor, is as clear as the sun on a cloudless day. You must put an end to his extravagance, and convince him to return the money to its rightful owners."

But the anger coursing through Rhadopis's veins prevented her from understanding exactly what it was the queen was saying, for her passions were aroused and she was filled with resentment. "What really saddens you," she said cruelly, "is that you see the gold directed with Pharaoh's affections toward my palace."

The queen shuddered, and she began to shake. "How repulsive," she cried.

"Nothing will come between me and His Majesty," said Rhadopis angrily and with pride.

Silence stayed the queen's tongue. She felt utter despair and her pride was deeply wounded. She could see no point in remaining any longer, and she rose to her feet and turning her back to the woman, she went on her way, pained, sad, and so furious that she could hardly see the way in front of her.

Rhadopis gulped for air, and leaned her spinning head on her palm, lost in sad and apprehensive thoughts.

A Glimmer of Light

Rhadopis sighed from deep in her wounded heart, and said to herself, "How I regret that I have become heedless of the world. But still it refuses to forget me or to leave me at peace now that I am cleansed of my past and those hoards of men." Dear Lord, were the priests really accusing her palace of consuming their stolen wealth? Were they really scourging her love with tongues of flame? She had huddled inside her palace contentedly, lost touch with everyone, and never stepped outside into the real world. She had no idea that her name was bandied about with such resentment on the tongues of these zealots who were using her as a ladder to reach up high enough to touch her worshipful lover. She did not think the queen was exaggerating, even if more than one motive had driven her to speak, for she had known for some time that the priests were concerned that Pharaoh would seize their lands, and she had heard with her own ears at the festival of the Nile those people shouting the name of Khnumhotep. There was no doubt that beyond the quiet, beautiful world that she inhabited was another more clamorous world, in which cauldrons were bubbling with affliction and resentment. She felt gloomy after long months of peace and serenity the like of which she had never experienced in her entire life. She felt her ribs curving compassionately around her lover, streaming with love and affection, and out of the depths of this sudden and unexpected grief that had come upon her, she remembered what Ani had said one day about the pharaonic guard being the only force the king could rely on, and how she had asked herself in alarm why His Sacred Majesty did not conscript soldiers, or mobilize a strong and powerful army.

She spent the whole day in her chamber, depressed, and did not go to the summer room as was her wont to sit for the sculptor, Benamun. She could not bear the thought of meeting anybody, nor sitting motionless in front of the young man's insatiable eyes. She saw no one until evening time, and she did not taste rest until she saw her worshipped lover come through the door of her bedchamber, trailing his flowing garments. She sighed from the depths of her heart as she opened her arms and he hugged her to his broad chest as he did every time, and planted on her face the happy kiss of greeting. Then he sat down by her side on the couch and waxed lyrical about the beautiful memories the view of the Nile had brought back to his mind as it had borne his barge just a moment earlier.

"Where is the beautiful summer?" he said to her. "Where are those nights spent awake, when the barge cuts through the dark still brow of night, when we lie in the cabin and succumb to passion in the cool breeze, listening to the music of the songstresses and watching with dreamy eyes the graceful movements of the dancers?"

She was unable to keep up with his reminiscences, but she did not want him to feel alone in an emotion or a thought and she said, "Do not rush, my darling. Beauty is not in the summer, nor in the winter, but in our love, and you will find the winter warm and gentle so long as the flame of our love burns."

He laughed his raucous laugh, and his face and body shook. "What a beautiful thing to say. My heart desires such wit more than all the glory in the world. But tell me, what do you think about some hunting? We shall go out into the mountains tomorrow and run after the gazelles, and amuse ourselves until our ravenous spirits are sated."

Her mind had begun to wander. "May your will be done, my darling."

He looked at her carefully, and realized at once that her tongue was speaking to him but her heart wandered far away.

"Rhadopis," he said, "I swear to you by the falcon that brought our hearts together, some thought steals your mind from me today."

She looked at him through two sad eyes, unable to say a word. Concern came over his face and he said, "My intuition was correct. Your eyes do not lie. But what is it you are holding back from me?"

She sighed from the depths of her heart, and as her right hand played unwittingly with his cloak, she said softly, "I wonder at our life. How much we are oblivious to what is around us, as if we were living in a deserted and uninhabited world."

"We are well to do so, my darling. What is the world to us other than endless noise and false glory? We were lost for so long before love guided us. What is it that unsettles you?"

She sighed again and said sadly, "What use is sleep to us if all around people are awake and cannot close their eyes."

He frowned, and a fleeting light shone in his eyes, and he knew in his heart that something was bothering her. "What is it that saddens you, Rhadopis?" he asked worriedly. "Share your thoughts with me, for have we not talked enough about things other than love?"

"Today is not like yesterday," she said. "Some of my slaves who were walking in the market related to me how they saw a group of angry people muttering that your wealth was being spent on this palace of mine."

Pharaoh's face showed anger, and he saw the specter of Khnumhotep hovering over his calm and peaceful paradise, clouding its serenity and disturbing its security. His anger intensified and his face turned the color of the Nile during the inundation, and he said to her in a trembling voice, "Is that what troubles you, Rhadopis? Woe be unto those rebels if they do not cease their transgression. But do not let it spoil our happiness. Pay no attention to their wailing. Leave them be and think solely of me."

He took her hand in his and squeezed it gently and she looked at him and said beseechingly, "I am worried and sad. It pains me that I should be a cause for people to denounce you. It is as if I feel a mysterious fear, the essence of which I cannot comprehend. A person in love, my lord, is quick to fear at the least cause."

"How can you be afraid when you are in my arms?" he asked her unhappily.

"My lord, they eye our love with envy, and resent this palace for its love and tranquility and comfort. Often have I said to myself in my sadness and inquietude, 'What has the gold that my lord lavishes upon me to do with love?' I will not deny to you that I have come to hate the gold that incites people against us. Do you not think that this palace will still be our paradise even if its floors were torn bare and its walls disfigured? If the glitter of gold will distract their eyes, Your Majesty, then fill their hands with it so that they go blind, swallowing their tongues."

"Do not say such things Rhadopis. You are reminding me of a matter I hate to hear about."

"Your Majesty," she pleaded, "it is about to envelop the sky of our happiness. Remove it with a single word."

"And what word might that be?"

She thought he was beginning to yield and see sense. "To give them back their lands," she said happily.

He shook his head violently. "You do not know anything about the matter Rhadopis," he insisted. "I spoke, but my word has not been respected; it has been implemented reluctantly, and they have not silenced their protests. They continue to threaten me and giving in to them is a defeat I will not accept. I would rather die than allow that. You do not know what defeat means to my soul. It is death. If they were victorious over me and took what they desired, you would find me a stranger, pathetic and pitiful, unable to live or to love."

His words penetrated to her heart and she held his hands more tightly. She felt her body tremble. She could bear anything, but not that he be incapable of life or love. She relinquished her desire, and regretted her beseeching, and in a quivering voice she exclaimed, "You shall never be conquered. Never."

He smiled at her tenderly. "Nor shall I err or falter, nor shall you be the fate that brings disgrace upon me."

A hot tear slipped from beneath her trembling eyelids.

"You shall never be disgraced," she said breathlessly, "you shall never be defeated."

She leaned her head against his chest, and let herself be lulled to sleep by the beating of his heart. In her slumber she felt his fingers playing with her hair and her cheeks, but she did not find peace for long, for one of the thoughts that had darkened her day tugged at her mind, and she looked up at him with worried eyes.

"What is the matter?" he asked.

She hesitated before she spoke. "It is said that they are a

strong party, with great sway over the hearts and minds of the people."

He smiled: "But I am stronger."

She paused a moment then said, "Why do you not conscript a powerful army that would be at your command?"

The king smiled and said, "I see that your misgivings are getting the better of you once again."

She sighed with irritation, "Did it not reach my ear that people are whispering among themselves that Pharaoh takes the money of the gods and spends it on a dancer? When people come together their whisper becomes a loud cry; like evil it will flare up."

"What a pessimist you are, seeing evil everywhere."

But she asked him again, pleading, "Why do you not summon the soldiery?"

He looked at her for a long time, thinking, then said, "The army cannot be called up without a reason."

He appeared angry and continued, "They are confused and misguided. They feel that I am displeased with them. If I announce conscription they will be alarmed. Maybe they would rise up desperately to defend themselves."

She thought for a moment, then, in a dreamy voice, as if she were talking to herself, she said, "Make up a pretext and summon the army."

"Pretexts make themselves up by themselves."

She felt desperate, and lowered her head sadly, her eyes closed. She was not asking for anything, but suddenly, in the utter darkness, an auspicious idea jumped out at her. She was staggered and when she opened her eyes, joy shone in them. The king was astonished, but she did not notice, for she could scarcely contain her excitement. "I have found a reason," she said.

He looked at her questioningly.

"The Maasayu tribes," she continued.

He understood what she meant, and shaking his head in despair, muttered, "Their leader has signed a peace treaty with us."

She would not be put off. "Who knows what is happening over the border? The ruling prince there is one of our men. Let us send him a secret message with a trustworthy messenger informing him to claim there is revolt and fighting in his province and send to us for help. We will spread his call throughout the land, you will summon the army and they will come to you from the North and South to gather under your banner. That will fix your broken wing and be your sword unsheathed. Thus shall your word remain supreme and obedience to your will be enforced."

Pharaoh listened to her in amazement, and wonder too, because the idea had never occurred to him. Although he had not thought much about the formation of a strong army when military circumstance did not require it, and had believed, and still did believe, that the mutterings of the clergy could not reach the level of danger that would require a large army to crush it, he had come to believe that the absence of such an army suited the people and tempted them to raise petitions, and voice aloud their complaints. He found Rhadopis's simple idea the perfect opportunity and he was taken by it with all his heart. And when he was taken by something, he would dedicate himself to it and be preoccupied with it, and focus on it with an obsession verging on madness, heedless of all else. For this he looked into her eyes, delighted. "What an excellent idea, Rhadopis," he said. "An excellent idea."

"It is what my heart tells me," she said curiously elated. "It is easy to accomplish, as easy as foregoing this kiss from your beloved mouth. All we must do is say nothing."

"Yes, my darling. Do you not see how your mind, like your heart, is a precious treasure? Truly, all we have to do is remain silent and choose a trustworthy messenger. You can leave that to me."

"Who might your messenger to Prince Kaneferu be?" she asked.

"I will choose a chamberlain from my loyal men."

She did not trust his vast palace, not for any rational reason, but because of her heart's aversion to the place in which the queen dwelled. She could not express her misgivings at all, but she had no idea who the messenger should be if he were not from the palace. To make matters worse, she fully understood that if the secret were exposed, the consequences would be too serious to even contemplate. She was about to despair and abandon altogether the sensitive and perilous project, when suddenly she remembered the child-like young man with the happy eyes who was working in the summer room. With the memory came a strange reassurance, for he was sincere and naïve and pure. His heart was a temple in which he offered to her rituals of worship, morning and night. He was her messenger; he was trustworthy. Immediately she turned to Pharaoh and said confidently, "Let me choose the messenger myself."

The king was amused. "What a nuisance you are today. Not your usual self at all. Who shall you choose, I wonder?"

"My lord," she reminded him humbly, "a person in love has many fears. My messenger is the artist who is decorating the summer room. In his age he is a young man but in his soul he is a child. He has the heart of a chaste virgin. He is totally devoted to me, and his most obvious advantage is that he will not arouse suspicion, and he knows nothing. It is far better for us if the person who bears our message knows nothing of its grave and serious contents. If we do not know fear, we can pass through all perils unscathed."

The king nodded in agreement: he hated to say no to her. As far as Rhadopis was concerned, the clouds had dispersed, even if it was not in the way she had originally intended. She was delighted and gave free reign to her joy, confident that soon she would be able to forget the world and live in her palace of love, leaving its protection to a mighty army, in the face of which all would be powerless.

Her head bowed with dreams and the beauty of her hair delighted the king. He adored her hair and his fingers dallied at the knot and untied it, and it cascaded down over her shoulders. He held it in his hands and breathed it deep into his nostrils, and buried his head and face in it, playfully, until they were both completely hidden by it.

The Messenger

The next morning broke and the air was cold. The sky was wrapped in robes of cloud, white and incandescent above the source of the sun, like an innocent face whose expression announces the inner thoughts, while the distant horizon was darker as if the tails of night lingered still as it withdrew.

A great task awaited her, but her heart was not inclined toward it, nor was the purification she had undergone that day at the temple pleased with it. Had she not sworn to wash away the past with all its stains? And here she was, waiting to deceive Benamun, and to play with his emotions in order to serve her love and bring her goal to fruition. She did not hesitate in the slightest though, for she was in a race against time. Her love meant more to her than anything else and she was prepared to use bitter cruelty for its sake. She left her chamber for the summer room, supremely confident. It would not require much guile to seduce Benamun. It would be easy.

She walked in on her tiptoes and found him looking at her picture, singing a song that she used to sing on evenings long ago:

If your beauty works miracles,
Then why can it not cure me?

She was taken aback by his singing, but she made use of the opportunity and sang the rest of the verse:

Am I playing with something I have no knowledge of?
The horizon is hidden behind the clouds,
I wonder if you are the one
Who's saved some love for my heart.

The young man turned to her, startled, bewitched. She met him with a sweet laugh and said, "You have a beautiful voice. How have you managed to hide it from me all these days?"

The blood rushed to his cheeks, and his lips trembled with consternation as he reacted to her kind affection with amazement.

She understood what he was thinking and she continued her enticement. "I see you enjoying a song, and neglecting your work," she said.

A look of denial appeared on his face, and he pointed to the picture he had engraved and mumbled, "Look."

The picture had become a beautiful face, almost lifelike. "How gifted you are, Benamun," she said in admiration.

He breathed a sigh of relief. "Thank you, my lady."

Then, steering the conversation toward her intention, she said, "But you have been cruel to me Benamun."

"I? How my lady?"

"You have made me look oppressive," she said, "and I so wanted to look like a dove."

He was silent, and did not say a word. She interpreted his silence to suit her purpose, and said, "Did I not say you have been cruel to me? How do you see me, Benamun? Oppressive, cruel, and beautiful as in this image you have made? What a picture it is. I am amazed how the stone speaks. But you imagine that my heart does not feel, just like this stone, do you not? Do not deny it. That is your belief. But why, Benamun?"

He did not know what to say. Silence overcame him. She was putting her ideas into his mind, and he believed them and was drawn toward her as he grew more muddled and confused.

"Why do you think I am cruel, Benamun?" she went on. "You believe in appearances, because by your nature you cannot conceal that which stirs in your breast. I have read your face like the page of an open book. But we possess another nature, and openness loses us the sweet taste of victory, and spoils the most beautiful things the gods have created for us."

Young Benamun asked himself in bewilderment what she could possibly mean, and whether or not he should understand from her speech what her words actually implied. Had she not been sitting there before him every day, her eyes and mind forever distracted? She had not sensed the fire raging in his being then. What had made her change? Why was she saying these delicious words to him? Why was she coming so near the sweet secrets that burned in his heart? Did she really mean what she was saying, did she really mean what he had understood her words to mean?

Rhadopis moved another step forward. "Ah, Benamun," she said. "You are being cruel to me. It is clear from the silence with which you answer me."

He gazed at her in bewilderment and tears of joy almost flooded his eyes. He knew for certain his thoughts had been correct. "There are not enough words in the world to express what I feel," he said in a trembling voice.

She breathed a sigh of relief that she had loosened the

knot on his tongue, and said dreamily, "What need have you of words? You will not say anything I do not know. Let us ask the summer room, for she has seen us for months and we have left in her body a trace of our hearts forever. Yes, here you have learned a solemn secret."

She looked into his face for a short moment then she said, "Do you know, Benamun, how I learned the secret of my heart? It was by way of a surprising coincidence. I have a personal letter I want to send to someone in a distant place, and to send it with a messenger I can rely on, someone my heart trusts. I was sitting alone, reviewing in my mind different people, men and women, slaves and freemen, and at each one I would feel uneasy, that they were not right for the task, then, I do not know why, my mind wandered to this room, and all of a sudden I remembered you, Benamun. My mind was assured and my heart at peace. Indeed, I felt something even deeper than that. Thus did I learn the secret of my heart."

The young man's face was awash with joy and he felt happiness almost to the point of delirium. He dropped to his knees before her and cried out from the depths of his heart, "My lady."

And placing her hand on his head she said tenderly, "That is how I knew the secret of my heart. I wonder how I did not know it from long ago."

"My lady," said Benamun, lost in his trancelike state, "I swear the night witnessed me convulsed with anguish, and now the dawn is here, greeting me with a breeze of sweet-scented joy. The words you have uttered have brought me out of darkness into light, transported me from the gloomy depths of despair to a magical sensation of happiness. I can love myself again after I was on the brink of perdition. You are my happiness, my dream, my hope."

She listened to him, sad and silent. She felt he was reciting a fervent prayer, as though he were floating in an ignorance of naïve, sacred dream. She was quiet for a while, feeling some pain and regret, but she did not give in to the emotions he had stirred in her heart with his rapture, and deviously she said, "I am surprised that I did not know my heart for so long, and I wonder at the coincidences that did not apprise me of its secret until I needed to send you on a mission far away. It is as if they led me to you, and deprived me of you at one and the same time."

"I will do whatever you will with my heart and soul," he said in a tone that was like worship.

After a moment's hesitation she asked, "Even if what I want is for you to travel to a land you will only reach with great difficulty?"

"The only difficult thing will be not seeing you every morning."

"Let it be a temporary absence. I will give you a letter you will keep by your breast. You will go to the governor of the island with a word from me. He will direct you on your way and smooth out any difficulties.

"You will travel with a caravan, not a single one of whom shall know what is by your breast until you reach the governor of Nubia and deliver the dispatch into his hand. Then come back to me."

Benamun felt a new joy mingled with feelings of dignity and pride. Her hand was nearby and he fell upon it with his mouth and kissed it passionately. She saw him tremble violently when his lips touched her hand.

On her way back, the feeling of sadness returned, and she asked herself, "Would it not have been more merciful to let His Majesty choose the messenger than for me to play with the heart of this boy?" Nevertheless, he was happy. Her lying words had made him so. Indeed, he was in a state that even the happiest of people would envy. She need not be sad as long as he did not know the truth, until, that was, she tired of resorting to falsehood.

The Letter

That same evening, Pharaoh came waving a folded letter in his hand, his face beaming with satisfaction. As she looked curiously at it, she wondered if it would bring her idea to a successful conclusion and direct events in accordance with her dreams. The king unfolded the letter and read it out with a happy glint in his eye. It was addressed to Prince Kaneferu the governor of Nubia, from his cousin, the pharaoh of Egypt. In it he explained his troubles and his desire to muster a huge army without arousing the suspicions or fears of the clergy. He requested the prince to send to Egypt a letter with a trustworthy messenger, calling for urgent assistance to defend the borders of the southern provinces and to suppress an imaginary rebellion, claiming it was the Maasayu tribes who had stoked its fires and swept through the towns and villages.

Rhadopis folded it up again and said, “The messenger is ready.”

The king smiled. “The letter is prepared.”

She was lost in thought for a moment, then asked, “I wonder how they will receive Kaneferu’s letter?”

“It will shake all their hearts,” said the king in a tone of conviction. “It will shake the hearts of the priests themselves and the governors will call for the conscription of men from every corner of the land, and soon enough the army our hope depends on will come to us, fully mustered and equipped."

She was delighted, and impatiently she asked him, "Shall we wait long?"

"We have a month to wait while the messenger makes the journey and returns."

She thought for a moment, and counted on her fingers, then said, "If your reckoning is correct, his return will coincide with the festival of the Nile."

The king laughed. "That is a good omen, Rhadopis, for the festival of the Nile is the anniversary of our love. It shall be an occasion of victory and reassurance."

She too was optimistic, believing dearly in the prosperity of that day, which she truly considered to be the birth of her happiness and love. She was convinced that the return of the messenger on that day was not just coincidence, but rather a prudent orchestration from the hand of a goddess who was blessing her love and was sympathetically disposed toward her hopes.

The king looked at her in wonder and admiration, then kissed her head and said, "How precious your head is. Sofkhatep is most impressed with it, as indeed he is most impressed with your brilliant idea. He could not resist telling me what a simple solution it was to a complex problem, like a pretty flower growing from a twisted stalk, or branches all knotted and gnarled."

She had been under the impression that he had kept the plan a secret and had told no one about it, not even the loyal prime minister, Sofkhatep. She asked him, "Does the prime minister know of our secret?"

"Yes," he said simply. "Sofkhatep and Tahu are as close to me as my mind and heart. I hide nothing from them.

Tahu's name rang in her ears, and her face became sullen, and a look of apprehension appeared in her eyes.

"Does the other know of it?" she asked.

The king laughed. "How wary you are, Rhadopis. But know that I do not trust myself with a thing I would not trust them with."

"Your Majesty," she said, "my misgivings would not extend to those you trust so implicitly."

Nevertheless, she could not help remembering Tahu at the hour of his last farewell. His harsh voice echoed in her ears as he ranted on in fury and despair, and she wondered if he might still not harbor some grudge.

But these dark thoughts had no chance to play on her heart, as she forgot herself between the arms of her beloved.

The next morning the messenger, Benamun Ben Besar, came wrapped in his cloak, his cap pulled down to his ears. His cheeks were red and his eyes shone with the light of heavenly joy. He prostrated himself in front of her in silent submission and humbly kissed the edge of her robe. She stroked his head with her fingertips and said tenderly, "I shall never forget, Benamun, that it is for me that you are leaving this abode of peace and tranquility."

His beautiful innocent face looked up at her, and in a trembling voice he said, "No labor is too great for your sake. May the gods help me to bear the pain of separation."

She smiled, saying, "You will return happy and refreshed. And in the joys of the future you will forget all the pains of the past."

He sighed, "Blessed be those who carry in their hearts a happy dream to keep them company in their loneliness and moisten their parched mouths."

Rhadopis beamed at him and picked up the folded letter and placed it in his hand. "I do not think I need tell you how careful you must be," she said. "Where will you keep it?"

"Under my shirt, my lady, next to my heart."

She handed him another smaller letter. "This is a letter to Governor Ani, so that he will help you on your way and arrange for you a place on the first caravan to leave for the South."

Then it was time to bid farewell. He swallowed; he was upset and confusion and longing showed in his face. She held out her hand to him and he hesitated a moment before placing it between his own. His palms trembled as if he was touching burning fire, then he held her so tightly to his breast that his heat and pulse flowed into her. At last he pulled away and disappeared through the door. She watched him helplessly as she mumbled fervent prayers.

Why not? For he had placed next to his heart the hope on which her very life depended.

Tahu's Delirium

The waiting was bitter as soon as it began, for she was plagued by a nagging doubt and she wished that the king had not divulged the secret of the letter to a single soul. The great trust the king placed in his two most loyal servants did not detract from her torment. Her misgivings were not based on absolute doubt, but rather on some apprehension that made her wonder what would happen if the men of the priesthood got wind of the content of the letter. Would they think twice before defending themselves against such an evil plot? O Lord! The secret of the letter divulged. It was too terrible to think about. No sane, patriotic mind could dare to comprehend how terrible. She felt a shiver run down her spine and she shook her head violently to cast the dark forebodings from her mind, and she whispered to her conscience to soothe it, "Everything will go according to the plan we have worked out. There is no need to stir up these fears, they are only the doubts of a heart so much in love that it knows not sleep nor rest."

But no sooner had she put her doubts at bay than her imagination drifted once again to hover round her fears: she saw Tahu's angry face contorted with agony and heard his hoarse voice, pained and wounded. She suffered greatly for her fears but she did not dare to interpret them, or remove the mystery that shrouded them.

She wondered if she was right to fear Tahu, or to think ill of him. All indications seemed to suggest that he had forgotten. But could he do something that he had, of his own accord, sworn not to? He could no longer knock at her door since it had become sacred and prohibited. All he could do was submit and obey, but that did not mean he had forgotten or was to be trusted.

She wondered if any remnants of the past still clung to his heart. Tahu was a stubborn bully, and love might transmute in his heart into concealed resentment, ready to wreak revenge when the occasion presented itself. Still, despite her turmoil, she did not forget to be just to Tahu, and she recalled his loyalty and his unswerving dedication to his lord. He was a man of duty who would not be led astray by desire or temptation.

Everything suggested that she should relax, yet she was plagued with misgivings. The messenger had left her palace only hours before; how then was she to wait for a month or more? She was at her wits' end, when suddenly the thought occurred to her to invite Tahu to come and meet her. She would not have dreamed of the idea the day before, but today it reassured her and she felt inclined to pursue it, forced along in the same way one is forced to embrace a danger one fears, but cannot deflect or escape from. She thought about it, unsure for a moment which course to take, then she said to herself, "Why not invite him and talk to him to see what his heart conceals. Perhaps I will be able to guard against his malice, if there is malice to be guarded against, and I shall save Tahu from himself, and save His Majesty from his evil." Her desire had turned into a determination that would accept no delay and seized her with all its might until she could think of nothing else. She immediately called Shayth and ordered her to go to Commander Tahu's palace and summon him.

Shayth went off while her mistress waited nervously in the reception hall. She had no doubt that he would accept her invitation. As she waited, it dawned on her how nervous she was, and she compared herself now to how strong and unfeeling she had been in the past. She realized that from the moment she had fallen in love she had turned into a weak and nervous woman whose sleep was haunted with ridiculous delusions and false fears.

Tahu came as she had expected. He was dressed in his official uniform, which reassured her somewhat, as if he were telling her that he had forgotten Rhadopis, the courtesan of the white palace, and that he was now in audience with the friend of his lord and majesty, Pharaoh.

The commander bowed his head in reverence and respect, and speaking quietly and without the slightest trace of emotion, said, "May the gods make happy your days, my venerable lady."

She examined his face, saying, "And your days too, noble commander. I thank you for accepting my invitation."

Tahu bowed again. "I am at your command, my lady."

He looked the same as he had before, strong, sturdy, and copper-skinned, but it did not escape her searching glance that some change had come over him that eyes other than hers would not have observed. She discerned upon the man's face a withered look that had dimmed the sparkle in his eyes and had quenched the all-encompassing spirit that once effused from his face. She was worried that the reason might be the events of that strange night they had parted ways almost a year ago. How awful it was! Tahu had been like a swirling wind; now he was like stagnant air.

"I have invited you, Commander," she said, "to congratulate you on the great trust placed in you by the king."

The commander seemed surprised and said, "Thank you, my lady. It is an old favor, bestowed upon me by the gods."

Forcing a smile, she said slyly, "And I thank you for the fine praise you lavished upon my idea."

The man thought for a moment before recalling, "Perhaps my lady means the brilliant idea that her lofty mind inspired?"

She nodded, and he continued, "It is a wonderful idea, worthy of your outstanding intelligence."

She showed no sign of pleasure, and said, "Its success guarantees the power and sovereignty of His Majesty, and peace and stability for the kingdom."

"That is true without doubt," said the commander. "That is why we greeted it with such enthusiasm."

She looked deep into his eyes and said, "The day will soon come when my idea will need your strength and power to bring it to fruition, to be crowned with victory and success."

Tahu bowed his head and said, "Thank you for your valued trust."

The woman was silent for a moment. Tahu was dignified, composed, and serious, not as she had known him in the past. She had not expected from him otherwise, and now she sensed trust and reassurance in his presence. She felt a burning impulse to bring up the old matter and to ask him to forgive her and forget, but words failed her. Her bewilderment got the better of her and she was afraid she would say the wrong thing. Reluctant and confused, she abandoned the idea. Then, thinking at the last moment to announce to him her good intentions in another way, she held out her hand, and smiled as she said, "Noble commander, I extend to you the hand of friendship and appreciation."

Tahu placed his rough hand against her soft and tender palm. He seemed moved, but he did not answer. Thus ended their short, crucial encounter.

On his way back to his boat he asked himself frantically why the woman had invited him. He gave free rein to the emotions he had stifled in her presence, flying into a rage as the color faded from his face and his body shook. Before long he had completely lost his mind, and as the oars plied the surface of the water he swayed like a drunkard, as if returning from a battle defeated, his wisdom and honor in shreds. The palm trees lining the shore seemed to dance wildly and the air was thick with choking dust. The blood rushed through his veins, hot and impassioned, poisoned with madness. He found a jug of wine on the table in the cabin and he poured it into his mouth. The drink made him reckless and moody and he threw himself down onto the couch in a state of abject despair.

Of course he had not forgotten her. She was concealed in some deep hidden recess of his mind, forever shut away by consolation, patience, and his strong sense of duty. Now that he had seen her for the first time in a year, the hidden deposit in his soul had exploded and the flames had spread to consume his entire being. He felt tormented by shame and despair, his pride slaughtered. Now he had tasted ignominy and defeat twice in the same battle. He felt his unbalanced head spinning as he spoke furiously to himself. He knew why she had gone to the trouble of summoning him. She had invited him to find out if she could trust his loyalty, to put her heart at rest regarding her beloved lord and majesty. In order to do so she had feigned friendship and admiration. How strange that Rhadopis, capricious and cruel, was suffering pain and anguish, learning what love is, and what fears and pains come in its wake. She feared some treachery from Tahu who once had clung to the sole of her sandal like dust and she had shaken him off in a moment of boredom and disgust. Woe to the heavens and the earth, woe to all the world. He was filled with an unspeakable despair that crushed his proud and mighty spirit to powder. His anger was violent and insane. It set his blood on fire and pressed on his ears so that he could hardly hear a sound, and it stained his eyes so that he saw the world a blaze of red.

As soon as the boat docked at the steps of the royal palace he strode off and, oblivious to the greetings of the guards, staggered up the garden toward the barracks and the quarters of the commander of the guard. Suddenly he found Prime Minister Sofkhatep walking toward him on his way back from the king's chambers. The prime minister greeted him with a smile. Tahu stood before him expressionless, as if he did not know him. The prime minister was surprised and asked, "How are you, Commander Tahu?"

"I am like a lion that has fallen into a trap," he replied with strange haste, "or like a tortoise lying upturned on top of a burning oven."

Sofkhatep was taken aback. "What are you saying? What likens you to a lion in a trap, or a tortoise on an oven?"

"The tortoise lives for a long time," said Tahu as if in a daze. "It moves slowly, and is weighed down by a heavy load. The lion shrinks back, roars, springs violently, and finishes off his prey."

Sofkhatep gazed into his face in amazement, saying, "Are you angry? You are not your usual self."

"I am angry. Would you deny me that, venerable sir? I am

Tahu, lord of war and battle. Ah, how can the world put up with this ponderous peace? The gods of war are parched and I must one day quench their burning thirst."

Sofkhatep nodded his head, in order to humor the commander. "Ah, now I understand, Commander. It is that fine Maryut vintage."

"No," said Tahu firmly. "No. Truly, I have drunk a cup of blood, the blood of an evil person it seems, and my blood is poisoned. But there is worse to come. On my way here, I encountered the Lord of Goodness sleeping in the meadow and I plunged my sword into his heart. Let us go to battle, for blood is the drink of the fearless soldier."

"It is the wine, no doubt," said Sofkhatep in dismay. "You should return to your palace at once."

But Tahu shook his head in disdain. "Be very careful, Prime Minister. Beware of corrupted blood, for it is poison itself. The tortoise's patience has run out, and the lion will pounce."

With that he went on his way, oblivious to all that was around him, leaving Sofkhatep standing there in a daze.

The Waiting

Pharaoh's palace, the palace of Biga, and the government house all waited impatiently for the return of the messenger. Yet they felt confident about the future. Each day that passed brought Rhadopis closer to victory, and hope glowed warmly in her breast. This optimistic mood may have continued uninterrupted had not the prime minister received an ominous letter from the priests. Sofkhatep generally ignored such letters, or felt obliged to show them to the queen, but this time he perceived a serious escalation. Not wishing to incur the ire of his lord for concealing it, even though showing it to him would provoke a certain amount of anger, he met Pharaoh and read him the letter. It was a solemn petition signed by all the clergy, with the high priests of Ra, Amun, Ptah, and Apis at their head, requesting His Majesty to restore the temple estates to their owners, the worshipped gods who protect and watch over Pharaoh, and affirming at the same time that they would not have submitted their petition if they had found any reason that would necessitate the appropriation of the lands.

The letter was strongly worded, and Pharaoh was furious. He tore it up into pieces and threw it on the floor. "I will respond to them soon enough," he shouted.

"They are petitioning you as one body," said Sofkhatep. "Before they were petitioning as individuals."

"I will strike them altogether, so let them protest the way their ignorance dictates."

Events however were moving quickly. The governor of Thebes sent word to the prime minister that Khnumhotep had visited his province and received a tumultuous welcome from the populace and the priests and priestesses of Amun alike. Cries had gone up in his name and the people had called for the rights of the gods to be preserved and upheld. Some even went further, and weeping, cried out, "Shame, the wealth of Amun is spent on a dancer!"

The prime minister was grievously saddened, but not for the first time his loyalty overcame his reluctance, and he tactfully informed his lord of the news. As usual the king was angry, and said regretfully, "The governor of Thebes watches and listens but can do nothing."

"My lord, he has only the force of the police," said Sofkhatep sadly, "and they are of no use against such large numbers of people."

"I have no choice but to wait," said the king, irritated. "Truly, by the Lord, my pride is bled dry."

A cloud of affliction settled over glorious Abu, and drifted into the lofty palaces and halls of government. Queen Nitocris stayed in her chambers, hostage of her confinement and loneliness, suffering the pangs of a broken heart and wounded pride as she watched events with sad and sorry eyes. Sofkhatep received all this news with a dejected heart, and would say sadly to taciturn and miserable Tahu, "Have you ever seen such rebellious unrest in Egypt? How sad it is."

The king's happiness had turned to anger and wrath. He did not taste rest unless he lay in the arms of the woman to whom he had surrendered his soul. She knew what plagued him. She would flirt with him and comfort him and whisper in his ear, "Patience," and he would sigh and say bitterly, "Yes, until I have the upper hand."

Still the situation deteriorated. The visits of Khnumhotep to the provinces increased. Wherever he went he was greeted by enthusiastic crowds, and his name rang out up and down the country. Many of the governors were gravely concerned, for the matter was placing serious strain on their loyalty to Pharaoh. The governors of Ambus, Farmuntus, Latopolis, and Thebes met to consult with one another. They decided to meet the king, and they headed for Abu and asked for an audience.

Pharaoh received them officially with Sofkhatep present. The governor of Thebes approached Pharaoh, uttered the greeting of humble veneration and loyalty, and said, "Your Majesty, true loyalty serves no purpose if it is simply an emotion in the heart. Rather it must be combined with sound advice and good works, and sacrifice if circumstance demands it. We stand before a matter in which honesty may expose us to displeasure, but we are no longer able to silence the stirring of our consciences. Therefore we must speak the truth."

Pharaoh was silent for a moment then said to the governor, "Speak, Governor. I am listening to you."

The man spoke with courage. "Your Majesty, the priests are angry. Like a contagion, their anger has spread among the people who listen to their speeches morning and evening. It is because of this that all agree on the necessity of returning the estates to their owners."

A look of vehemence appeared on the king's face. "Is it right that Pharaoh should yield to the will of the people?" he said furiously.

The governor continued, his words bold and direct: "Your Majesty, the contentment and well-being of the people is a responsibility with which the gods have entrusted the person of Pharaoh. There is no yielding, only the compassion of an able master concerned for his slaves."

The king banged his staff on the ground. "I see only submission in retreat."

"May the gods forbid that I refer to Your Majesty as submissive, but politics is a churning sea, the ruler a captain who steers clear of the raging storm and makes full use of good opportunity."

The king was not impressed with his words and he shook his head in stubborn contempt. Sofkhatep requested permission to speak, and asked the governor of Thebes, "What proof do you have that the people share the sentiments of the priests?"

"Yes, Your Excellency," said the governor without hesitation. "I have sent my spies around the region. They have observed the mood of the people at close quarters and have heard them discussing matters they should not."

"I did the same thing," said the governor of Farmuntus, "and the reports that came back were most regrettable."

Every governor spoke his piece, and their statements left no doubt about the precariousness of the situation. Thus ended the first such meeting of its kind ever seen in the palaces of the pharaohs.

Immediately the king met with his prime minister and the commander of the guard in his private wing. He was beside himself with rage, threatening menace and intimidation. "These governors," he said, "are loyal and trustworthy, but they are weak. If I were to take their advice I would lay open my throne to ignominy and shame."

Tahu quickly seconded His Majesty's opinion, and said, "To retreat now is clearly defeat, my lord."

Sofkhatep was thinking about other probabilities. "We

must not forget the festival of the Nile. Only a few days remain before it begins. In truth, my heart is not happy at the thought of thousands of irate people gathered in Abu."

"We control Abu," Tahu was quick to point out.

"There is no doubt about that. But we should not forget that at the last festival certain treacherous cries were heard, even though at that time His Majesty's wish had still not been realized. This year we should expect other, more vociferous cries."

"All hope hangs on the return of the messenger before the festival," said the king.

Sofkhatep continued to consider the matter from his own point of view, for in his heart he believed in the proposal of the governors. He said, "The messenger will come soon and he will read his message for all to hear. No doubt the priests, having courted the favor of their lord and believing that they once again enjoyed their ancient rights, will be more enthusiastically inclined to accept mobilization, for even if my lord were to take the upper hand and dictate his desire, there is none who can refuse to do his will."

The king took umbrage at Sofkhatep's opinion, and feeling isolated and alone even in his private wing, he hastened to the palace of Biga, where loneliness never followed him. Rhadopis did not know what had happened in the latest meeting and her mind was less troubled than his. Still, she found no difficulty reading the telling expression on his face and sensed the anger and vexation that churned in his heart. She was filled with trepidation and she looked at him questioningly, but the words piled up behind her lips, afraid to come out.

"Have you not heard, Rhadopis?" he grumbled. "The governors and ministers are advising me to return the estates to the priests, and to content myself with defeat."

"What has urged them to pronounce this counsel?" she asked nervously.

The king related what the governors had said and what they had counseled him to do and she grew sadder and more nervous. She could not restrain herself from saying, "The air grows dusty and dark. Only grave danger would have led the governors to reveal their opinions."

"My people are angry," said the king scornfully.

"Your Majesty, the people are like a ship off course without a rudder, which the winds carry wherever they will."

"I will knock the wind out of their sails," he said ominously.

Fears and doubts returned to plague her, and her patience betrayed her for a moment as she said, "We must seek recourse to wisdom and willingly step back awhile. The day of victory is near."

He looked at her curiously. "Are you suggesting that I submit, Rhadopis?"

She held him to her breast for his tone had hurt her, then she said, her eyes overflowing with fervent tears, "It is more proper for one about to take a great leap to first crouch down. Victory hinges upon the outcome."

The king moaned, saying, "Ah, Rhadopis, if you do not know my soul, then who can know it? I am one who, if coerced to bend to a person's will, withers with grief like a rose battered by the wind."

Her dark eyes were touched by his words and she said with deep sadness, "I would gladly sacrifice myself for you, my darling. You will never wither as long as my breast waters you with pure love."

"I shall live victorious every moment of my life, and I shall never give Khnumhotep the pleasure of saying that he humiliated me for even an hour."

She smiled at him sadly and asked, "Do you wish to govern a people without at times resorting to subterfuge?"

"Surrender is the subterfuge of the incapable. I shall remain, while I am alive, as straight as a sword upon whose blade the forces of the traitors will be smashed."

She sighed sadly and regretfully and did not try to win him round. She was content with defeat in the face of his anger and pride, and from that moment she began to ask herself incessantly, "When will the messenger return? When will the messenger return? When will the messenger return?"

How tedious the waiting was. If those who desire knew the torment of waiting as she now did, they would prefer abstinence in this world. How she counted the hours and minutes and watched the sun rise and waited for its setting. Her eyes ached from long looking at the Nile as it wound its way from the South. She reckoned the days with bated breath and throbbing heart, and often cried out when she could stand the apprehension no more, "Where are you, Benamun?" Even love itself she tasted as one distracted, far away in thought. There would be no peace of mind, no rest until the messenger returned with the letter.

The days elapsed, slowly dragging their intolerable heaviness, until one day she was sitting engrossed in her thoughts, when Shayth burst into the room. Rhadopis raised her head and asked her, "What pursues you, Shayth?"

"My lady," said the slave girl eagerly, panting for breath, "Benamun has returned."

Joy engulfed her and she jumped to her feet like a startled bird as she called out, "Benamun!"

"Yes, my lady," said the slave girl. "He is waiting in the hall. He asked me to inform you of his arrival. How he has caught the sun on his travels."

She ran in great bounds down the stairway to the hall and

found him standing there waiting for her to appear. A burning desire shone in his eyes. She seemed to him like a flame of joy and hope, and in his mind he had no doubt that her joy was because of him and for him. Divine rapture flowed over him and he threw himself at her feet like one in worship. Wrapping his arms around her legs passionately and with great affection, and falling upon her feet with his mouth, he said, "My idol, my goddess, I dreamed a hundred times I kissed these feet, and now my dreams are come true."

Her fingers played with his hair as she said gently, "Dear Benamun, Benamun, have you really returned to me?"

His eyes shone with the light of life. He thrust his hand inside his jerkin and pulled out a small ivory box and opened it. Inside it was dust. "This dust is some of that which your feet trod upon in the garden," he said. "I gathered it up with my hands and kept it in this box. I carried it with me on my journey and would kiss it every night before surrendering to sleep and place it against my heart."

She listened to him, anxious and perturbed. Her feelings had turned away from the words he spoke and as her patience expired, she asked with a calmness that masked her apprehension, "Do you not bear anything?"

He thrust his hand into his jerkin once again and took out a folded letter which he held out to her. She took receipt of it with trembling hand. She was awash with happy feelings and she felt a numbness in her nerves and a languor in her powers. She cast a long look at the letter and held it tightly in her hand. She would have forgotten Benamun and his ardent passion had not her glance fallen upon him, and she recalled an important matter. "Did not a messenger from Prince Kaneferu come with you?" she inquired.

"Yes, my lady," said the youth. "He it was who carried

the message during our return. He is waiting now in the summer room."

She was unable to stand there any longer, for the joy that flooded her senses was enemy to stillness and immobility, and she said, "May the gods be with you for now. The summer room awaits you and untroubled days lie ahead for us."

Off she ran carrying the letter, calling out for her beloved lord from the deepest recesses of her heart. Were it not for her sense of propriety she would have flown to him in his palace, like the falcon had done before, to bear him the glad tidings.

The Meeting

The day of the festival of the Nile arrived, and Abu welcomed revelers from the farthest reaches of the North and South. Ballads rang out on the city's air and its houses were adorned with banners and flowers and olive branches. The priests and the governors greeted the rising sun on their way to Pharaoh's palace where they joined the great royal cavalcade, which was due to set off from the palace in the late morning.

As the assembled notables waited in one of the chambers for the king to come down, a chamberlain entered, and saluting them in the name of the king, announced in a stentorian voice: "Venerable lords, Pharaoh wishes to meet with you at once. If you would be so kind as to proceed to the pharaoh's hall."

All greeted the chamberlain's declaration with unconcealed surprise, for it was the custom that the king received the men of his kingdom after the celebration of the festival, not before it. Confusion was etched on their faces as they asked one another, "What grave matter could it be that occasions a meeting which violates the traditions?"

Nevertheless they accepted the invitation and moved obediently to the splendid and magnificent reception hall. The priests occupied the seats on the right-hand side while the governors sat opposite them. Pharaoh's throne commanded the scene between two rows of chairs arranged in wings to seat the princes and ministers.

They did not have to wait long before the ministers entered with Sofkhatep at their head. They were followed after a while by the princes of the royal household who sat to the right of the throne, returning the greetings of the men who had stood up to salute them.

Silence fell and seriousness and concern appeared on every face. Each was alone with his own thoughts, asking himself what lay behind the calling of this extraordinary meeting. The entrance of the seal bearer interrupted their musing and they gazed at him with undivided attention, as the man called out in his solemn voice, announcing the coming of the king: "Pharaoh of Egypt, Light of the Sun, Shadow of Ra on the Earth, His Majesty Merenra II."

All rose and bowed until their foreheads almost touched the floor. The king entered the hall august and dignified, followed immediately by the commander of the guard Tahu, the seal bearer, and the head chamberlain of Prince Kaneferu, governor of Nubia.

Pharaoh sat down on the throne and said in a solemn voice, "Priests and governors I salute you, and I grant you permission to be seated."

The bowed forms straightened gently up and the men sat down amidst a silence so deep and absolute that it made the very act of breathing a hazardous venture. All eyes were directed toward the owner of the throne, all ears eager to hear his words. The king sat upright and spoke, shifting his eyes from one face to another but settling on none. "Princes and ministers, priests and governors, flower of the manhood of Upper and Lower Egypt, I have invited you in order to take your counsel on a grave matter that pertains to the well-being of the kingdom and the glory of our fathers and forefathers. Lords, a messenger has come from the South. He is Hamana, grand chamberlain of Prince Kaneferu, and he bears a grave and weighty message from his lord. I was of the opinion that my duty required me to call you without delay, in order to peruse it and take counsel on its ominous contents."

Pharaoh turned to the messenger and signaled to him with his staff. The man took two steps forward and stood in front of the throne. Pharaoh said, "Read them the message."

The man unfolded the letter he held in his hands and read in a resonant and impressive voice: "From Prince Kaneferu, governor of the lands of Nubia, to his Royal Highness Pharaoh of Egypt, Light of the Shining Sun, Shadow of the Lord Ra, Protector of the Nile, Overlord of Nubia and Mount Sinai, Master of the Eastern Desert and the Western Desert.

"My lord, it grieves me to bring into the hearing of your sacred personage unfortunate news about treacherous and dishonorable happenings that have befallen the territories of the crown in the marshes of southern Nubia. I had, my lord, being reassured by the treaty concluded between Egypt and the Maasayu tribes, and given the unbroken calm and improved security that had ensued after the sealing of that agreement, ordered the withdrawal of many of the garrisons stationed in the desert to their main bases. Today, an officer of the garrison foot soldiers came to me and informed me that the leaders of the tribes had split asunder the rod of obedience and reneged on their oaths. They swept down out of the night like thieves, attacked the garrison barracks, and wrought a savage slaughter upon them. The contingent fought back desperately against forces that were a hundred times their number or more until they fell to the last man on the field of valor. The tribes laid waste to the country all around then headed north toward the land of Nubia. I saw it wise not to overstretch the limited forces at my disposal, and to direct my concern at fortifying our defenses and fortresses so that we might stall the advancing foe. By the time this letter reaches my lord our troops will have already engaged the aggressor's vanguard. I await my lord's command, and remain at the head of my warriors, waging battle for the sake of my lord Pharaoh and my country Egypt, my motherland."

The messenger finished reading out the letter but his voice continued to resonate in many hearts. The governors' eyes were ablaze, sparks flying from them, and a wave of violent unrest shook their ranks. As for the priests, they had knitted their brows and their faces were impassive, turned into frozen statues in a soundless temple.

Pharaoh was silent for a moment, allowing the consternation to reach its peak. Then he said, "This is the letter which I called you to take counsel upon."

The governor of Thebes was at the forefront of the zealous ones. He rose to his feet, bowed his head in salute, and said, "My lord, it is a solemn dispatch indeed. The only answer is a summons to mobilization."

His words found an enthusiastic welcome in the hearts of the governors, and the governor of Ambus stood up and said, "I second that opinion, my lord. There is only one answer and that is swift mobilization. How otherwise when beyond the southern borders our valiant brethren are sorely beset by the enemy? And though they are steadfast, we should not forsake them nor tarry in their aid."

Ani was thinking about the consequences that might encroach upon his sphere of influence. He said, "If those barbarians lay waste to the land of Nubia they will threaten the border without a doubt."

The governor of Thebes recalled an old opinion he had long hoped would one day be vindicated: "I was always of the opinion, my lord, that the kingdom maintain a large and permanent army that would enable Pharaoh to undertake his commitments in defending the well-being of the motherland and our possessions beyond the borders."

Ardor grew strong in all the commanders' flanks, with many calling for mobilization. Others hailed Prince Kaneferu and the Nubian garrison. Some of the governors were sorely moved and said to the king, "My lord, it gives us no pleasure to celebrate the festival while death bears down upon our valiant brethren. Give us permission to depart and muster our men at arms."

Pharaoh remained silent in order to hear what the priests might say. These latter too took recourse to silence while spirits calmed, and when the hubbub in the ranks of the governors had finally died down, the high priest of Ptah rose to his feet and, with remarkable composure, said, "Would my lord grant me permission to pose a question to the emissary of His Majesty Prince Kaneferu?"

"You have my permission, priest," said the king stiffly.

The high priest of Ptah turned toward the emissary and said, "When did you quit the lands of Nubia?"

"Two weeks since," replied the man.

"And when did you reach Abu?"

"Yesterday evening."

The high priest turned to face Pharaoh and said, "Revered and worshipful king, this matter is indeed most confusing, for this venerable messenger came to us yesterday from the South bearing news that the leaders of the Maasayu had rebelled, and yet that same yesterday a delegation of Maasayu elders arrived from the farthest reaches of the South to proffer the obligatory rites of obedience to their lord Pharaoh, and to offer to your Highness their profound gratitude for the bounty and peace you have bestowed upon them. How pressing therefore is our need of one who can shed some light upon this mystery."

It was a bizarre declaration, and one that no one had expected. It provoked great amazement and wonder. All heads were convulsed by a violent commotion while the governors and priests exchanged questioning and unruly looks, and the princes whispered amongst themselves. Sofkhatep was struck dumb and he gazed at his lord in utter dismay. He saw Pharaoh's hand tighten its grip upon his staff, and clench it so firmly that the veins bulged on his forearm and the color drained from his face. The man was afraid that anger had taken control of the king so he asked the high priest, "Who informed you of this, Your Holiness?"

"I saw them with my own eyes, my Lord Prime Minister," replied the man softly. "I visited the temple of Sothis yesterday and its priest presented to me a delegation of black men who said they were Maasayu chiefs and had come to perform the rites of obedience to Pharaoh. They stayed the night as guests of the high priest."

"Is it not the case that they are from Nubia?" said Sofkhatep, but the high priest was adamant. "They said they were Maasayu. In any event, there is a man here among us—he is Commander Tahu—who has clashed with the Maasayu in many wars and knows all their headmen. If Your Majesty would be so gracious as to order that these chiefs be summoned to his sacred court, then perhaps their testimony will remove the veil of confusion from our eyes."

The king was in a pronounced state of dread and rage, yet he had not the slightest inkling how to forestall the high priest's proposal. He felt all faces scrutinizing him with anxious expectation as they waited in suspense, and at length he said to one of the chamberlains, "Go to the temple of Sothis and call the visiting chiefs."

The chamberlain departed obediently and all waited, utterly still with consternation drawn on every face, as each man stifled a heartfelt desire to question his neighbor and listen to his thoughts. Sofkhatep remained alarmed and apprehensive, as thoughts raced incessantly through his mind and he snatched worried and bewildered glances from his lord, with whom he sympathized deeply in this dreadful hour. The minutes passed, ponderous and agonizing, as if they were being torn from their very flesh. From his throne the king surveyed the restless governors and the priests, who sat heads bowed. His eyes were barely able to conceal the emotions doing battle in his heart. Then all imagined they heard a commotion borne upon the air from afar. Each man emerged from his inner dialogue and pricked up his ears as the hubbub neared the square outside the palace. It was the clamor of voices cheering and hailing, which as they drew nearer, grew steadily louder and more intense until they seemed to fill the hall, all mingling together, none distinguishable above the rest, yet still the long palace courtyard stood between them and the assembled grandees. The king ordered one of the chamberlains to step onto the balcony and ascertain the cause of the disturbance. The man disappeared for a moment then hastily returned, and, inclining toward Pharaoh's ear, said, "Throngs of the populace are filling the square, surrounding the chariots which come bearing the chieftains."

"And what is their call?"

"They are saluting the loyal friends from the South and the peace treaty."

Then the man wavered for a moment before continuing in a whisper, "And, my lord, they are hailing the treaty-maker, Khnumhotep."

The king's face paled with indignation, and he felt some great malice driving him into a corner as he wondered how he could call a people who were feting the Maasayu chieftains and hailing the peace treaty, to go to war with the very same Maasayu. He awaited the approaching dignitaries with a growing sense of exasperation, despair, and gloom.

An officer of the guard announced the arrival of the leaders, and the door was thrown wide open. The delegation entered, preceded by their headman. There were ten of them, strapping of form, naked except for a loincloth girded about their waists, and on their heads wreaths of leaves. Together they prostrated themselves on the ground and crawled forward until they reached the threshold of the throne where they kissed the ground in front of Pharaoh. The king held out his staff to them and each man put his lips to it in submission. The king granted them permission to stand and they rose to their feet in awe, whereupon their leader said in the Egyptian tongue, "Sacred Lord, Pharaoh of Egypt, Deity of the Tribes, we have come to your abode that we might offer to you the manifestations of humiliation and subjugation, and to give praise for the favor and blessings you have bestowed upon us, for thanks to your mercy, we have eaten delicious food and we have drunk sweet and fragrant water."

Pharaoh raised his hand in benediction.

All faces were turned to him, willing him to ask them some news of their land. "From which clans are you?" asked the vanquished king.

"O Sacred Splendor," said the man, "we are chieftains of the Maasayu tribes who pray for your splendor and glory."

The king was silent awhile, and declined to ask them anything about their followers. He had had enough of the place and those in it and said, "Pharaoh thanks you, loyal and faithful slaves, and blesses you."

He extended his staff and they kissed it once again. Then they retraced their steps, their forms bent double so that their foreheads almost touched the floor.

Anger flared up in Pharaoh's breast, and he sensed a painful realization in his heart that the clergy arrayed before him had struck him a mortal blow in some arcane battle that only he and they could comprehend. His wrath welled up inside him and his rage overflowed as he fumed at his defeat and said in a peremptory tone, "I have here an epistle whose veracity is unassailed by doubt, and whether the rebellious tribes pay homage to these men or not, one thing remains certain: there is a revolt, there are insurgents, and our troops are surrounded. The governors' enthusiasm returned unabated, and the governor of Thebes said, "My lord, it is divine wisdom that flows upon your tongue. Our brethren await reinforcements. We should not waste our time in discussion when the truth is staring us in the face."

"Governors," said the king vehemently, "I exempt you this day from participating in the celebration of the Nile festival, for before you lies a more sublime duty. Return to your provinces and muster men-at-arms, for every minute that is lost shall cost us dear."

With these words the king rose to his feet, thereby indicating the termination of the assembly. All rose at once and bowed their heads in reverence.

The Shout in the Crowd

Pharaoh made for his private wing and summoned his two loyal men, Sofkhatep and Tahu, to join him. They were quick to oblige, for they were severely shaken by what had happened, and under no illusion whatsoever as to the gravity of the situation. They found the king as they had expected, furious and enraged, pacing the room from wall to wall as he ranted insanely. Suddenly aware of them, he cast them a sidelong glance, and said, with sparks flying from beneath his eyelids, "Treason. I smell foul treason in this nasty air."

Tahu stalled, then said, "My lord, while I do not deny on my part a certain pessimism and misgiving, my intuition would not go as far as such a grand supposition."

The king went berserk, stamping his foot on the ground, shouting, "Why did that damned delegation turn up? And how did they come today? Today of all days?"

Sofkhatep, immersed in his thought and woes, said, "I wonder if it might not just be an unhappy and bizarre coincidence?"

"Coincidence!" stormed the king terrifyingly. "No! No! It is wicked treason. I can almost see its face—veiled, the head deviously bowed. Nay, Prime Minister, those folk did not come by coincidence, but rather were sent here by some design to say peace if I were to say war. Thus has my enemy dealt me a severe blow, just as he stands before me professing loyalty."

Tahu's face turned pale, and a poignant look appeared in his eyes. Sofkhatep, not contending the king's view, lowered his head in despair and said, as if he were talking to himself, "If it is treason, then who is the traitor?"

"Indeed," said the king as he shook his fist in the air. "Who is the traitor? Is there then a mystery that cannot be unraveled? Of course there is not. I do not betray myself. Sofkhatep and Tahu would not stab me in the back. Nor would Rhadopis. There is none left save that malicious messenger. Alas, Rhadopis is deceived."

A glint shone in Tahu's eye as he said, "I will drag him here and wring the truth from his mouth."

The king shook his head, saying, "Slowly, Tahu, slowly. The villain is not waiting for you to go and arrest him. Perhaps, as we speak, he is enjoying the fruits of his treachery in a safe place known only to the priests. How was the deception accomplished? I cannot think, but I will swear by the Lord Sothis that they learned of the letter before the messenger set off. Wasting no time, they sent an emissary of their own. Mine came back with the dispatch, theirs with the delegation. Treachery, villainy! I am living like prisoner among my own people. May the gods curse the world and all mankind."

The two men did not make a sound, out of sadness and pity. Tahu detected a look of distress in his lord's eyes and, wanting to instill some fresh hope into their dire mood, he said, "Let our consolation be that we shall strike the decisive blow."

The king was exasperated. "And how shall we aim this blow?" he asked.

"The governors are on their way to the provinces to muster soldiers."

"And do you imagine that the priests will stand, hands bound, before an army they know has been assembled to eradicate them?"

Sofkhatep was laboring under a formidable burden, and though he was willing to accept the king's prognosis, he wished to get the weight off his chest so he said, as if he were making a wish, "Perchance our opinion is a fallacy, and what we deem treason is no more than coincidence, and these dun clouds will scatter at the least cause."

Pharaoh flared up again at this show of sympathy. "The image of those priests with their heads lowered still hangs in my mind. I have no doubt they harbor an awesome secret in their hearts. There is not a single reason to suspect otherwise. When the high priest rose to speak, he challenged the zeal of the governors with ease, delivering his word with unbounded confidence. Perhaps even now he is speaking with ten tongues. How despicable treason is. Merenra will not live his life at the beck and call of the clergy."

Tahu, sorely riled at his lord's distress, said, "My lord, you have at your command a battalion of guards of strapping build, each one a match for a thousand of their men, each of whom would gladly sacrifice himself for his lord's sake."

Pharaoh brushed him aside and, sprawling out on a sumptuous divan, surrendered to the torrid thoughts that surged through his head. Might not his hope be realized in spite of all these woes? Or would his project fail once and for all? What a historic hour in his life this was. He stood at the crossroads between glory and humiliation, power and collapse, love and loss. He had refused to yield over the estates as a matter of principle. Would he soon find himself compelled to capitulate in order to preserve his throne? Ah, that day would never come, and if it did, he would never allow himself to be abased. He would remain to his dying breath noble, glorious, and mighty. In spite of himself he let out a mournful sigh and said, "The pity of it, that treason should lie in fortune's way."

Sofkhatep's voice put an end to his musing. "My Lord, the time of the pageant is at hand."

Pharaoh peered at him like one roused from a deep slumber and muttered, "Is that so?" Then he stood up and strode over to the balcony, which looked out over the grand courtyard of the palace. The company of chariots stood in ranks at the ready, and in the distance, waves of clamorous revelers could be seen breaking into the square. Upon this teeming world he cast a pallid glance and returned to where he had been standing. Then he entered his chamber and disappeared for a brief time. He re-emerged wearing the leopard skin insignia of the priesthood and the double crown. All present made ready to depart but before they could make a move, a palace chamberlain entered, saluted his lord and said, "Lord Tam, commissioner of the Abu police, requests permission to stand before his lord."

The king and his two counselors, remarking the signs of consternation on the man's face, granted it. The chief constable saluted his lord and, with great haste and much perturbation, said, "My lord, I have come to humbly beseech your sacred personage to refrain from proceeding to the temple of the Nile."

The two men's hearts skipped a beat as the king said anxiously, "And what has led you to make this recommendation?"

Panting heavily, the man replied, "I have this very hour arrested a large number of people who were directing malicious chants at a noble personage held in high esteem by my lord, and I fear the same chants may be repeated during the procession."

He king's heart quivered and caldrons of rage boiled in his blood as he asked the man in a hesitating voice, "What did they say?"

The man swallowed nervously and, with some embarrassment, said, "They shouted, 'Down with the whore! Down with her who plunders the temples!'"

At this the king flew into a rage and cried out in a voice like thunder, "What sore affliction! I must strike the blow that will rid me of them once and for all or else my whole being will explode!"

The man went on, panic in his voice, "The miscreants resisted my men, and pitched battles took place between them and us and for a while there was chaos and disarray, at which point more evil and seditious cries went up."

The king ground his teeth in exasperation and disgust as he asked, "What else did they say?"

The man looked down at the floor and said almost in a whisper, "The insolent villains violated one more exalted."

"I?" said the king in disbelief.

The man fell back in silence and the color drained out of his face. Sofkhatep was unable to contain himself and cried out, "How can I believe my ears?"

And Tahu stormed, "This is a madness that cannot be imagined."

Pharaoh laughed nervously and, with bitter rancor in his voice, said, "How did my people mention me, Tam? Speak, man. I order you."

The police commissioner said, "The scoundrels cried out, 'Our king is frivolous. We want a serious king.'"

The king laughed a laugh like the first, and said sarcastically, "What a pity. Merenra is no longer worthy to sit on the throne of the clergy. What else did they say, Tam?"

The man spoke so softly that his voice was scarcely audible, "They called out the name of Her Majesty, Queen Nitocris, many times, my lord."

A sudden glint flashed in the king's eye and the name Nitocris echoed softly between his lips, as if he had recalled something old that had long since been forgotten. The two advisers exchanged a look of alarm. Pharaoh sensed their consternation, and the quandary of the police commissioner. Pharaoh did not want to make of the queen a subject for bitter talk, but he could not help wondering with some dismay what the queen's feelings toward these slogans might be. He was utterly depressed and felt a violent wave of anger, defiance, and recklessness wash over him. Addressing Sofkhatep, he said brusquely, "Is it time to depart?"

But Tam said in bewilderment, "Will my lord not desist from going?"

And the king said, "Are you not listening to me, Prime Minister?"

Sofkhatep was perturbed, and said humbly, "In a moment, my lord. I thought my lord was resolved not to go."

But the king said with a calmness like that which comes before the storm, "I shall go to the temple of the Nile, passing through the infuriated multitudes, and we shall see what will come to pass. Return to your duties, Tam."

Hope and Poison

That same morning, Rhadopis was lounging on a sumptuous divan, dreaming. It was one of those rare days, bursting with festive joy and promising great victory for her. What happiness, what joy. This day her heart was like a pool of clear and fragrant water, flowers sprouting around its edges, and all about in the air nightingales chirping their sweet refrains. How joyous the world is! When would she receive the news of victory? When evening came and the sun began its journey to the underworld, and her heart commenced its own journey into the realm of abandonment with her darling beloved. How marvelous was evening time. Evening time, hour of the beloved, when he will come into her with his lithe figure and glowing youth, and wrap his sinewy arms around her slender waist, as he whispers her name softly in her ear with glad tidings of victory, saying, "The pain is over. The governors have gone on their ways to amass the soldiery. Now, let us see to our love." Ah yes, how beautiful evening time is.

And yet she hardly could believe that the day would pass. She had waited a month for the messenger to return and though the passing of that time had been grueling and intolerable, these few hours were crueler and more unsettling than anything she had experienced. Nevertheless, there was some relief mixed with her worry, and her fear was tempered by a touch of happiness. It was as if she wanted to pull the wool over Time's eyes and pretend the waiting did not exist. Her thoughts veered hither and thither until, in her wanderings, she alighted upon the lover kneeling in his temple, in the summer room. Benamun Ben Besar. How delicate he was, how sweet his presence, she mused, as she asked herself once again in dismay how she should reward him for the momentous service he had rendered her. He had flown on the wings of a dove to the farthest reaches of the South and had returned more swiftly than he went, borne by his passion, overcoming through it all obstacles along the way. At one point she had wondered in her confusion how she could get rid of him. But he had taught her with his contentment a wondrous love that did not know egoism or possessiveness or greed. He was satisfied with dreams and fantasies, for he was an idealistic youth, unschooled in the ways of the world. If he had coveted a kiss for example, she would not have known how to refuse him, and she would surely have offered him her mouth. But he coveted nothing, as if afraid to touch her lest he be consumed in mysterious flames. Or perhaps he did not believe that she was something that could be touched and kissed at all. He did not look upon her with the eye of a human being and he could not see that she was human too. He desired only to live in the radiance of her splendor like the plants of the earth live by the sun as it floats through the heavens.

She sighed and said, "Truly the world of love is a marvelous place." Her own love sprang exuberantly from the font of her being, for the force which attracted her to her lord was the very force of life itself, pristine and awesome. Benamun's love, however, was such as to shut out all reason for living, and he wandered astray, beyond sublime horizons, never announcing a trace of feeling save through his prodigious hands and sometimes on his hot and stumbling tongue. It was such a fragile love in some ways, moving like a phantom through a dream, and so strong in others, for it breathed life into solid rock. How could she contemplate getting rid of him when he did not bother her at all? She would leave him safe in his temple, depicting upon its silent walls the most beautiful embellishments to frame her ravishing face.

She cried out once again from the depths of her heart, "When is evening?" Damned Shayth. If she had stayed by her side she would have entertained her with her gossip and bawdy banter, but she had insisted on going to Abu to watch the pageant.

How beautiful memories can be. She remembered last year's festival, the day her luscious palanquin was born aloft and cut its way through the seething multitudes to see Pharaoh, the youth. When her eyes beheld him, he had moved her heart without her knowing it, and she had felt the sudden rush of love as something strange and unfamiliar, for so long had she lived with drought, that she thought it angry nervousness, or a spell breathed by a sorcerer. Then that eternal day, when the falcon soared off with her sandal, and the second day had hardly begun when Pharaoh visited her. From there, love had found its way into her heart. Her life had changed and the whole world had changed with it.

Now it was the second year, and here she was, holed up in her palace while the world feasted and made merry outside. She would not be destined to appear again except on the rarest of occasions, for Rhadopis was no longer the courtesan and dancer, but rather for a whole year now and forever after, she was the pulsating heart of Pharaoh. Her thoughts roamed here and there, but it was not long before they were inevitably drawn back to he who was uppermost in her mind, and she wondered what had happened at the extraordinary meeting that her lord had convened in order to have the message read out before it. Had the conference taken place and the assembled grandees rallied to the call, thereby bringing her cherished hope ever nearer to fulfillment? O Lord, when would evening come?

She grew tired of sitting and stood up to stretch her legs. She strolled over to the window that looked out upon the garden and cast her eyes over the spacious grounds. And there she remained until she heard a frenzied hand knocking on the door. With considerable irritation she turned round and saw her slave girl Shayth fling open the door and charge into the room, gasping for breath as her eyes darted back and forth and her chest rose and fell. Her face was pallid as if she had just risen from the bed of a long sickness. Rhadopis's heart beat faster and she was filled with dread as she asked her apprehensively, "Shayth, what is the matter?"

The slave tried to speak, but she burst into tears as she knelt in front of her lady, and clasping her hands to her breasts, she wept uncontrollably. Rhadopis was overcome with an intense perturbation, and she shouted, "What is wrong with you, Shayth?

"By God, speak woman! Do not leave me prey to confusion. I have hopes and I fear they will be dashed by some malicious conspiracy."

The woman breathed a deep sigh and, gulping for air as she spoke, said in a tearful sobbing voice, "My lady, my lady. They have flared up in open revolt."

"Who have?"

"The people, my lady. They are screaming things, angry and insane. May the gods tear out their tongues."

Her heart leapt into her mouth and in a trembling voice she said, "What are they saying, Shayth?"

"Alas, my lady, they have gone berserk and their poisonous tongues are ranting frightful things."

Rhadopis was out of her mind with terror and she shouted out sternly, "Do not torment me, Shayth. Tell me honestly what they were saying. O Lord!"

"My lady, they mention you in a very unflattering way. What have you done, my lady, that you so deserve their wrath?"

Rhadopis clasped her hand to her breast. Her eyes were wide with panic as she said in a halting voice, "Me? Are the people angry with me? Could they find nothing on this sacred day to take their minds off me? Dear Lord! What did they say, Shayth? Tell me the truth, for my sake."

The woman wept bitterly as she spoke. "The insane louts were crying out that you had made off with the money of the gods."

She let out a gasp from her stricken breast, and muttered woefully, "Alas, my heart is plucked out and quakes in fear. What I dread most is that the victory we anticipated is lost amid the uproar and the cries of rage. Would it not have been more worthy of them to ignore me out of respect for their lord?"

The slave struck her breast with her fist and wailed, "Not even our lord himself escaped their venomous tongues."

The terrified woman let out a scream of terror, and she felt a shudder rock the very foundations of her being. "What are you saying? Did they have the audacity to besmirch Pharaoh?"

"Yes my lady," sobbed the woman. "O the pity of it. They said, 'Pharaoh is frivolous. We want a serious king.'"

Rhadopis raised her hands to her head as if she were

shouting for help, her body was contorted with the severity of the pain and she threw herself desperately onto the divan as she said, "Dear Lord, what horror is this? How does the earth not quake, and the mountains crumble to dust? Why does the sun not pour down its fire upon the world?"

"It is quaking, my lady," said the slave. "It is quaking mightily. The populace is locked in violent combat with the police. Blood gushes and flows. I was almost trampled underfoot, and I ran for my life, oblivious to the fray, and I came down to the island in a skiff. My fears only increased when I saw the Nile heaving with boats, the people on board shouting the same slogans as those on the land. It was as if they had all agreed to come out at the same time."

She was overwhelmed with fatigue and a wave of choking despair crashed down on her and drowned her floundering hopes without mercy. She began to ask her grief-stricken heart, "What on earth has happened in Abu? How have these grievous events come to pass? What provoked the people and whipped them into such a frenzy? Was the message doomed to failure and her hope destined to die?" The air was thick with dust, gloomy and somber, and harbingers of imminent evil flew about in all directions. Her heart would not savor rest now, for mortal fear gripped it like a fist of ice. "O ye Gods, help us," she exclaimed. "Has my lord appeared before the citizenry?"

Shayth reassured her, saying, "No, he has not, my lady. He shall not quit his palace until his castigation has been visited upon the rebellious mob."

"Dear Lord! You do not know how he thinks, Shayth. My master is irascible, he will never stand down. I am so afraid, Shayth. I must see him, now."

The slave shook with fright as she said, "That is impossible. The water is covered with boats all packed to the brim with angry mobs, and the island guards are assembled on the bank."

She tore at her hair as she cried out, "Why is it that the world is closing in upon me, doors slammed shut in my face? I am tumbling down a dark well of despair. O my darling! How do you fare now at this moment? How can I come to you?"

Shayth said to solace her, "Patience, my lady. This dark cloud will pass."

"My heart is torn in pieces. I sense he is in pain. O my master, my darling! I wonder what events are transpiring now in Abu."

These woes overpowered her, all the pain burst open in her heart and her tears flowed fervently. Shayth was perturbed at this unfamiliar display, seeing the high priestess of love, luxury, and indulgence in floods of tears, wailing desperately as comatose with grief she pondered her dashed hopes that had been so real just minutes before. Her heart felt the icy blade of fear as she asked herself in alarm and trepidation, "Would they be able to coerce her lord against his will and deprive him of his happiness and his pride? Would they make her palace an object of their hatred and dissatisfaction?" Life would be unbearable if either of these nightmares came true. It would be better for her to put an end to her life if it lost its splendor and joy. Now Rhadopis, who once was courted by love and glory, was about to choose between life and death. She thought about her dilemma for a long time until at length the sadness brought to her a thought she had consigned to the deeper recesses of her memory. She was suddenly overcome with curiosity and she rose quickly and washed her face with cold water to remove any traces of weeping from her eyes. She said to Shayth that she wished to talk to Benamun about certain matters. The youth was engrossed in his work, as usual, oblivious to the unhappy events that were turning the world black. When he realized she was there, he walked toward her, his face beaming with joy, but he quickly fell silent. "By the truth of this ravishing beauty, you are indeed sad today," he said.

"Not at all," she replied, lowering her gaze, "just a little unwell, like a woman sick."

"It is very hot. Why do you not sit an hour by the edge of the pool?"

"I have come to you with a request, Benamun," she said abruptly.

He folded his arms across his chest as though saying, "Here I am, at your disposal."

"Do you remember, Benamun," she asked him, "you told me once of a marvelous poison concocted by your father?"

"Indeed I do," said the young man, surprise appearing upon his face.

"Benamun, I want a phial of that marvelous poison which your father named 'the happy poison.'"

Benamun's surprise grew more apparent, and he muttered questioningly, "What on earth for?"

In a tone as calm as she could manage, she said, "I was talking to a physician and he expressed interest in its regard. He asked me if I might be able to supply him with a phial, with which he might save the life of a patient. I promised him, Benamun. Will you now promise me in your turn to fetch it for me without further delay?"

It delighted him that she should ask him for whatever she wished and he said merrily, "You will have it in your hands in a matter of hours."

"How? Will you not have to go to Ambus to fetch it?"

"Not at all. I have a phial at my lodgings in Abu."

His announcement aroused her curiosity in spite of all her woes and she gazed at him in bewilderment. He lowered his eyes and his face reddened. In a low voice he said, "I went and brought it in those painful days when I was almost cured of my love and wallowed in deep despair. Had it not been for the affection you showed after that, I would now be in the company of Osiris."

Benamun went off to fetch the phial. She shrugged her shoulders contemptuously, and as she stood up to leave, she said, "I may resort to it instead of some more evil outcome."

Arrow of the People

Obeying his lord's command, Tam saluted and departed with confusion and fear drawn upon his countenance. The two men were left standing there alone, ashen-faced. Sofkhatep broke the silence with a plea. "I beseech you, my lord, refrain from going to the temple today."

Pharaoh could not stomach such advice and, knitting his brow in anger, he said, "Am I to flee at the first call that goes up?"

The prime minister said, "My lord, the populace are worked into a frenzy. We must take time to reflect."

"My heart tells me that our plan is headed for certain failure, and if I give in today I will have lost my dignity forever."

"And the people's anger, my lord?"

"It will die down and abate when they see me cut through their ranks in my chariot like a towering obelisk, facing peril head on, not surrendering or submitting."

Pharaoh began to pace up and down the room irascible and in a violent temper. Sofkhatep was silent, concealing his own rage. He turned to Tahu as if calling for help, but it was clear from the commander's ghostlike complexion, distant eyes, and heavy eyelids that he was swamped by his own woes. A profound silence fell over them, and all that could be heard were the king's footsteps.

A court chamberlain hurried nervously into the room, breaking their stillness. He bowed to the king and said, "An officer of the police requests permission to be granted an audience, my lord."

The king granted him permission, and he cast his two men a look to ascertain the effect of the chamberlain's words on their demeanor. He found them perturbed and ill at ease, and a wry smile formed on his lips as he shrugged his broad shoulders disdainfully. The officer entered, breathless from the effort and commotion. His uniform was caked with dust and his helmet battered and askew. It did not bode well. The man saluted and before being permitted to speak, said, "My lord! The citizenry is engaged in violent battle with the constables of the police. Many men have been killed on both sides, but they will overpower us if we do not receive substantial reinforcements from the pharaonic guard."

Sofkhatep and Tahu were horrified. They looked at Pharaoh and saw his lips were trembling with rage. "By every god and goddess in the pantheon," he roared, "these folk have not come to celebrate the festival!"

The officer had more to say: "Our spies have reported, my lord, that there are priests inciting the masses on the outskirts of the city, claiming that Pharaoh is using an imaginary war in the South as a pretext to muster an army with which to crush the people. The people, believing them, have grown enraged. If the police had not stood in their way they would have stormed the approaches to the sacred palace."

Pharaoh bellowed like thunder, "Doubt gives way to certainty. Pernicious treason has come to light. It is them, declaring their aggression and initiating the attack."

These were strange and unbelievable words that assailed their ears, and it appeared upon all their faces as if they asked incredulously, "Is this truly Pharaoh? And this the people of Egypt?" Tahu could stand it no longer, and said to his lord, "My lord, this is a baneful day, as if the forces of Darkness thrust it unnoticed into the cycle of time. It began with bloodshed and the Lord knows best how it will end. Command me to do my duty."

"What will you do, Tahu?" Pharaoh asked him.

"I will deploy the men-at-arms on the fortified defenses and I will lead out the company of chariots to meet the mob before they overcome the police and force their way into the square and the palace."

Pharaoh smiled mysteriously and was quiet for a while, then in a solemn voice, he said, "I will lead them myself."

Sofkhatep was aghast. "My lord," he blurted out.

The king struck his chest aggressively with his hands, saying, "This palace has been a stronghold and a temple for thousands of years. It will not become the base objective of every rebel who cares to raise his voice in protest."

The king removed the leopard skin and, throwing it aside in disgust, rushed into his chamber to don his martial attire. Sofkhatep was fast losing his nerve, and sensing dread and disaster, he turned to Tahu and in a commanding tone, said, "Commander, we have no time to lose. Be gone and make ready to defend the palace and await the orders that come to you."

The commander left the room followed by the police officer, while the prime minister waited for the king.

Events, however, were not waiting, and the wind carried a clamorous racket that grew ever louder and more defiant until it drowned out every other sound. Sofkhatep rushed over to the balcony that overlooked the palace courtyard and gazed out into the square beyond. From all around, masses of people were pouring into the square, shouting and clamoring, brandishing swords and daggers and clubs, as if they were the waves of a huge and powerful flood. Nothing but bare heads and flashing blades as far as the eye could see. The prime minister felt a shudder of dread. He looked below and saw the slaves in hurried commotion, sliding the huge bolts into place behind the great door. The infantry looked as sprightly as falcons as they ascended the towers that had been erected on the northern and southern ends of the outfacing wall. A large company of them moved into the colonnade that led down to the garden, carrying lances and bows. The chariots stayed back at the rear, drawn up in two long rows below the balcony in readiness to charge down the courtyard if the outer gate were breached.

Sofkhatep heard footsteps behind him. He turned round to see Pharaoh standing at the door onto the balcony in the uniform of the commander in chief. Upon his head was the double crown of Egypt. Sparks shot from his eyes and wrath was drawn upon his face like a tongue of flame. He spoke with fury and rage. "We are surrounded before we can make a move."

"The palace, my lord, is an impregnable fortress and stalwart warriors defend it. The priests will be routed in defeat."

Pharaoh was frozen to the spot. The prime minister moved back and stood behind him, whereupon they looked out together in doleful silence at the throngs of people so vast their numbers could not be counted as they poured toward the palace like wild beasts, brandishing their weapons menacingly and crying out in voices like thunder, "The throne belongs to Nitocris. Down with the frivolous king." The archers of the royal guard loosed their arrows from behind the towers and they hit their mark to deadly effect. The mob returned fire with a tremendous burst of stones, blocks of wood, and arrows.

Pharaoh nodded his head, and said, "Bravo, bravo, you rapacious people who come to overthrow the frivolous king. What anger is this? What revolution? Why do you brandish those weapons? Do you really want to plunge them into my heart? Well done, well done! It is a spectacle that deserves to be preserved on the temple walls for all eternity. Bravo, O People of Egypt."

The guards were fighting fiercely and valiantly, pouring down arrows like rain. Whenever one of them fell dead, another would take his place with death defiance, while the commanders mounted on horseback rode up and down atop the walls directing the battle.

As he beheld these tragic scenes he heard behind him a voice he knew only too well saying, "My lord."

He wheeled round astonished, and saw the one who had called him only two steps away. "Nitocris!" he exclaimed in wonder.

In a voice full of sadness the queen said, "Yes, my lord. My ears were rent with a foul screaming, the likes of which the Nile Valley has not heard before and I came to you, running, to declare my loyalty and to share your fate."

With these words she knelt down on her knees and bowed her head. Sofkhatep withdrew. The king took her by the wrists and lifted her to her feet as he gazed at her with bewildered eyes. He had not seen her since the day she had come to his wing, and he had reproached her in the cruelest manner. He was deeply hurt and embarrassed, but the cries of the people and the screams of the fighting men brought him back to his former state and he said to her, "Thank you, sister. Come, take a look at my people. They have come to wish me a happy feast day."

She lowered her eyes, and said with deep sorrow, "A monstrous blasphemy is that which they utter."

The king's sarcasm transformed itself into a raging bitter anger, and in tones swollen with disgust, he said, "A crazy country, choking air, polluted hearts, treachery. Treachery and treason."

The hair stood up on the back of the queen's neck at the mention of the word "treason," her eyes froze in dread, and she felt her breath imprisoned in her chest.

Was it possible that the mob's chanting her name had provoked some misgivings? Would her reward be for him to accuse her after her heart had grieved at his woes, and she had come of her own accord to he who had insulted her and treated her harshly? The very thought broke her heart, and she said, "The pity of it, my lord. There is naught I can do except to share your fate, but I can only wonder who the traitor might be, and how the treachery was devised."

"The traitor is a messenger to whom I entrusted a letter—he delivered it to my enemy."

Surprised, the queen said, "I have no knowledge of a letter, or of a messenger, nor do I think that there is time to inform me. I want nothing from you save that I appear by your side before the people who are clamoring for me so that they will know I am loyal to you, and that I stand against those who stand against you."

"Thank you, little sister. But there is no trick. All I must do is prepare for a noble death."

Then he grabbed her arm and walked her to his room of contemplation, pulling back the curtain that was drawn over its door, and they entered together into the sumptuous room. The interior was dominated by a niche carved in the wall, in which were set statues of the previous king and queen. The royal siblings walked over to the statues of their parents, and stood before them in silence and humility, peering with sad and melancholy eyes. As he looked at the statues of his parents, the king said in a heavy voice, "What do you think of me?"

He was silent for a moment as if he were waiting for an answer. His anxiety returned and he became angry with himself, then his eyes fixed on the statue of his father as he said, "You passed on to me a great monarchy and deep-rooted glory. What have I done with them? Hardly a year has passed since I came to the throne and already destruction looms. Alas, I have let my throne be trod underfoot by all and sundry, and my name is chewed upon every lip. I have made for myself a name that no pharaoh before me was ever called: the frivolous king."

The young king's head leaned forward, ponderous and forlorn, and he stared at the floor with darkened eyes, then raising them again to his father's statue, he muttered, "Perhaps you find in my life much to humiliate you, but my death will not shame you."

He turned to the queen and said to her, "Do you forgive my transgression, Nitocris?"

She could contain herself no longer and tears flooded from her eyes as she said, "I have forgotten all my troubles at this hour."

He was deeply agitated and said, "In harming you, Nitocris, I have dared to intrude upon your pride. I have wronged you and my stupidity has made the story of your life a sad legend which will be greeted with surprise and disbelief. How did it happen? Could I have changed the course my life was taking? Life has swamped me and an outlandish madness has possessed me. Even at this hour I cannot express my regret. How tragic that the intellect is able to know us and all our ridiculous trivialities, and yet appears incapable of rectifying them. Have you ever seen anything as ruthless and unsparing as this tragedy that afflicts me? Even so, the only lesson people will derive from it will be in rhetoric. Madness will remain as long as there are people alive. Nay, even if I were to begin my life anew I would err and fall once again. Sister, I am sick and tired of everything. What use is there in hoping? It is better if I bring on the end."

A look of resolve and unconcern came over his face as she asked him in a bewildered and nervous voice, "What end, my lord?"

And he said solemnly, "I am no mean degenerate. I can remember my duty after this long forgetfulness. What is the point of fighting? All my loyal men will fall before an enemy as numerous as the leaves of the trees, and my turn will inevitably come after thousands of my warriors and my people have been annihilated. Nor am I a timorous coward who, clutching at a faint glimmer of hope, will cling desperately to life. I will put an end to the bloodshed and face the people myself."

The queen was terrified. "My lord," she cried, "would you burden the consciences of your men with the ignominy of abandoning your defense?"

"Rather, I do not wish that they sacrifice themselves in vain. I will go out to my enemy alone that we may settle the score together."

She felt deeply frustrated. She knew his stubbornness and she despaired of changing his mind. Quietly and firmly she said, "I will be by your side."

He was shocked, and grabbing her by the arms, pleaded with her, "Nitocris, the people want you. They have chosen well. You are worthy to govern them, so stay with them. Do not appear by my side or they will say that the king is hiding behind his wife from the rage of the people."

"How can I abandon you?"

"Do it for my sake, and commence no work that will deprive me of my honor forever."

The woman felt confused, desperate, and deeply sad, and she cried out hopelessly, "What an awful hour this is."

"It is my wish," said the king, "carry it out in memory of me. Please, I beseech you, do not resist, for every minute that passes valiant soldiers are falling in vain. Farewell, kind and noble sister. I depart sure in the knowledge that you shall not be sullied with shame in this my final hour. One who has enjoyed absolute authority cannot be content with confinement in a palace. Farewell to the world. Farewell to the self and to pain. Farewell perfidious glory and hollow appearances. My soul has spit it all out. Farewell, farewell."

He leaned forward and kissed her head. Then he turned to the statues of his parents, bowed to them, and left.

He found Sofkhatep waiting in the outer lobby, motionless like a statue worn down since time immemorial. When he saw his lord, life stirred within him and he followed in silence, construing the king's exit to his own convenience and said, "My lord's appearance will instill a spirit of zeal in their valiant hearts."

The king did not answer him. They strode down the steps together into the long colonnade that ran down the garden to the courtyard. He sent for Tahu and waited in silence. At that moment, his heart was suddenly drawn to the southeast, where Biga lay, and he sighed from the depths of his heart. He had said farewell to everything except the person he loved the most. So, would he breathe his final breath before setting eyes upon Rhadopis's face and hearing her voice for the last time? He felt a poignant longing in his heart and a deep sadness. Tahu's voice saluting roused him from his troubled trance, and instantly, as if pushed by an irresistible power, he asked about the way to Biga, saying, "Is the Nile safe?"

His face drawn and drained of color, the commander replied, "No, my lord. They attempted to attack us from the rear in armed barges, but our small fleet repelled them without much effort. The palace will never be taken from that direction."

It was not the palace that worried the king. For that he bowed his head and his eyes clouded over. He would die before he cast a farewell glance upon that face, for which he had sold the world and all its glory. What was Rhadopis doing at this grievous hour? Had news reached her that her hopes were dashed, or did she wander still in vales of happiness, waiting impatiently for him to return?

Time did not permit him to surrender to his thoughts, and consigning his pains to his heart, he said to Tahu in a commanding tone, "Order your men to abandon the walls, cease fighting, and return to their barracks. Tahu was stunned with amazement and Sofkhatep, unable to believe his ears, said with some irritation, "But the people will break down the gate at any minute."

Tahu stood there, showing no sign of moving, so the king roared in a voice like thunder that rang terrifyingly down the colonnade, "Do as I command."

Tahu departed in a daze to effect the king's order, while Pharaoh walked forward with deliberate steps toward the palace courtyard. At the end of the colonnade he met with the company of chariots that had been deployed there in rows. Officers and men had seen him and their swords were drawn in salute. The king summoned the company commander and said to him, "Take your company back to its barracks and remain there until you receive further orders."

The commander saluted and, running back to his company, gave the order to the soldiers in a powerful voice. The chariots moved quickly and in orderly fashion back to their barracks in the south wing of the palace. Sofkhatep's limbs were trembling, and his feeble legs could hardly carry him. He had understood what the king intended to do, but he was unable to utter a single word.

The men-at-arms quit their positions in compliance with the dreadful order, and coming down from the walls and towers, they fell in under their standards and ran quickly back to their barracks behind their officers. The walls were now empty, and the courtyard and colonnades were deserted. Even the force of regular guards, whose duty it was to guard the palace during peacetime, had left.

The king remained standing at the entrance to the colonnade, with Sofkhatep to his right. Tahu came back out of breath and stood on Pharaoh's left, with a look upon his face like that of a fearsome specter. Both men wished to plead with the king and warmly beseech him, but the harsh look frozen upon his face dissipated their courage and they were compelled to silence. The king turned to them and said, "Why are you waiting with me?"

The two men were filled with great fear, and all Tahu could do was to utter a word of fervent sympathy: "My lord."

As for Sofkhatep, he said with unusual calmness, "If my lord orders me to forsake him I will obey his order without question, but I will put an end to my life immediately thereafter."

Tahu sighed with relief, as if the old man had come upon

the solution that had stubbornly evaded himself, and he mumbled, "You have spoken well, Prime Minister."

Pharaoh was silent, and did not say a word.

During this time violent and crushing blows had slammed into the great gate of the palace. No one had been bold enough to scale the walls, as if they were afraid, having been unsettled by the garrison's sudden withdrawal and imagining some mortal trap had been set for them. So they directed all their force at the gate, which was unable to withstand their pressure for long. The entire structure was wrought with convulsions as the bolts burst open and it came down with a mighty thud that sent violent shock waves through the earth. The clamoring hoards flooded in and spread throughout the courtyard like dust in a summer wind, surging forward violently as if engaged in combat. Fearing some unseen danger, those in front slowed down as much as they could, but still edging forward until they came within sight of the royal palace and their eyes fell upon the one standing at the entrance to the colonnade, the double crown of Egypt upon his head. They recognized him instantly and were taken aback by the sight of him standing there alone in front of them. The feet of those at the head of the mob clung fast to the ground and they raised their hands to halt the surging flood of people pouring down behind them, shouting into the throng, "Slowly, slowly."

A faint hope flickered in Sofkhatep's heart when he saw the fear that came over those at the front of the crowd, paralyzing their legs and causing them to avert their eyes. In his battered and exhausted heart he expected a miracle that would take the place of his black thoughts. But among the throng there were some conniving deviously against the wishes of Sofkhatep's heart, fearing that their victory might turn to defeat and their cause be lost forever. A hand reached out for its bow, nocked an arrow, took aim at Pharaoh and loosed the string. The arrow leapt out from the midst of the crowd and slammed into Pharaoh's upper chest, no power or wish could deflect it. Sofkhatep cried out as if it were he who had been hit. He held out his hands to support the king and they met Tahu's cold hands halfway. The king pursed his lips but no moan came out, nor any sigh. Knitting his brow, he mustered what strength remained in him to maintain his balance. Pain was drawn over his face and he quickly felt weak and drained. His eyes clouded over and he gave himself up to the arms of his two trusted men.

A terrible hush fell upon the front ranks and a heavy silence bound their tongues. Their panic-stricken eyes darted wary glances at the great man propped up by his two counselors, as he fingered the spot where the arrow had entered his chest, and warm blood flowed copiously from the wound. It was as if they could not believe their eyes, or as if they had attacked the palace for some other goal than this.

A voice from the rear tore through the silence, asking, "What is happening?"

Another responded in a more subdued tone, "The king has been killed."

The news spread like wildfire through the crowd, as the people repeated the words and exchanged looks of horror and confusion.

Tahu called a slave and ordered him to fetch a litter. The man ran off into the palace to return with a group of slaves carrying a royal litter. They set it down on the ground and all lifted Pharaoh and laid him gently down on it. The news spread inside the palace and the king's physician hurried out. The queen appeared behind him moving with hurried steps and in obvious distress. When her eyes alighted upon the litter and he who lay upon it, she ran to him in trepidation, and falling to her knees next to the physician, she said in a trembling voice, "Alas, they have stricken you, my lord, as was your desire."

The people beheld the queen and one of them cried out, "Her majesty the queen."

The heads of the dumbfounded populace all bowed in unison as if they were performing a communal prayer. The king started to come round from the effects of the initial shock, and opening his heavy eyes he looked weakly and quietly at the faces of those gathered round him. Sofkhatep was gazing into his face in a silent stupor. Tahu stood motionless, his face like the faces of the dead. The physician, having removed the shirt of mail, was examining the wound. As for the queen, her face wore an expression of anguish and pain and she said to the physician, "Is he not well? Tell me he is well."

The king was aware of her words, and he said simply, "It is not so, Nitocris. The arrow is fatal."

The physician wanted to remove the arrow, but the king said to him, "Leave it. There is no point in hoping for an end to this torment."

Sofkhatep was deeply moved and he said to Tahu with a great fury that completely changed the tone of his voice, "Call your men. Avenge your lord from these criminals."

The king seemed vexed, and raising his hand with great difficulty, he said, "Do not move, Tahu. Do my orders not matter to you now, Sofkhatep, as I lie here thus? There shall be no more fighting. Inform the priests they have achieved their goal and that Merenra lies on his deathbed. Let them go in peace."

A shudder ran through the queen's body as she leant to his ear and whispered, "My lord, I do not love to weep in front of your killers, but let your heart rest assured, by our parents and by the pure blood that runs in our veins, I will heap such revenge upon your enemies, that time will recount the tale of it for generations to come."

He smiled to her a light smile expressing his thanks and affection. The physician washed the wound, gave him a soothing potion to dull the pain, and placed some herbs around the arrow. The king gave himself up to the man's ministering hands but he felt that death was near and his final hour fast approaching. He had not forgotten, as life drained from him, the beloved face he longed to bid farewell to before his inevitable demise. An expression of yearning appeared in his eyes, and he said in a faint voice, oblivious to what was happening around him, "Rhadopis, Rhadopis."

The queen's face was close to his, and she felt a sharp blow pierce the membrane around her heart. A sudden dizziness took hold of her and she raised her head. He paid no attention to the feelings of those around him and he beckoned to Tahu, who stepped forward, and said to him hopefully, "Rhadopis."

"Shall I bring her to you, my lord?" he asked.

"No," replied the king feebly. "Take me to her. There is some life remaining in my heart, I want it to expire on Biga."

With deep uncertainty Tahu looked at the queen, who rose to her feet and said calmly, "Carry out my lord's desire."

Hearing her voice, and minding her words, the king said to her, "Sister, as you have forgiven me my sins, so forgive me this too. It is the wish of a dying man."

The queen smiled a sad smile and leaned over his brow and kissed it. Then she stepped aside to make room for the slaves.

Farewell

The boat slipped gently downstream toward Biga, the litter inside the cabin carrying its precious cargo. The physician stood at Pharaoh's head, and Tahu and Sofkhatep at his feet. It was the first time grief had reigned over the barge as it bore the slumbering, surrendering lord, the shadow of death hovering about his face. The two men stood in silence, their eyes never leaving the king's wan face. From time to time he would lift his heavy eyelids and look at them weakly, then close them again helplessly. Gradually the boat drew nearer to the island, docking eventually at the foot of the steps leading up to the garden of the golden palace.

Tahu leaned over and whispered in Sofkhatep's ear, "I think one of us should go ahead of the litter lest the shock prove too much for the woman."

At this terrible hour Sofkhatep did not care about the feelings of anyone, and he said abruptly, "Do what you think fit."

But Tahu stayed where he was, and seized by confusion and hesitation, he said, "It is terrible news. What person would know how to break it to her?"

Sofkhatep said decisively, "What are you afraid of, commander? He who has been tried as sorely as we have throws caution to the wind."

With these words Sofkhatep hurried out of the cabin, up the steps to the garden and down the path until he reached the pool, where he found the slave girl, Shayth, blocking his way. The woman was amazed to see him, for she knew him from the old days, and she opened her mouth to speak but he gave her no chance, and blurted out, "Where is your mistress?"

"My poor mistress," she said, "she can find no rest today. She's been going round the rooms and wandering through the garden till. . . ."

The man's patience wore thin and he interrupted her, "Where is your mistress, woman?"

"In the summer room, sir," she said, much offended.

He proceeded to the room with great haste, and entered, clearing his throat as he did so. Rhadopis was seated upon a chair with her head in her hands. When she felt him enter she turned round, and recognized him at once. She leapt sharply her feet and asked with grave concern and apprehension, "Prime Minister Sofkhatep, where is my lord?"

Such was his sadness that he spoke in a kind of trance, "He is coming shortly."

And she clasped her hand to her breast in joy, and said delightedly, "How I was tormented by fears for my master. News of the tragic rebellion reached me, then I heard nothing more and I was left alone with dark fears gnawing my heart. When will my master come?"

Then, suddenly, it occurred to her that he was not in the habit of sending a messenger ahead of him and she was seized with anxiety, and before Sofkhatep could utter a word she said, "But why has he sent you to me?"

"Patience, my lady," said the prime minister impassively. "No one has sent me. The grievous truth is that my lord has been wounded."

These last words rang weird and bloody in her ears and she stared in terror at the prime minister's desolate face as a trembling pathetic moan issued from deep in her lungs. Sofkhatep, whose sensitivity had been obliterated by grief, said, "Patience, patience. My lord will arrive borne on a litter, as was his wish. He has been struck by an arrow this perfidious day that dawned a feast and will end with dreadful obsequies."

She could not bear to linger in the room a moment longer, and she charged into the garden like a slaughtered chicken. But no sooner had she passed through the door than she stopped dead in her tracks, her eyes transfixed on the litter being borne toward her by the slaves. As she made way for them she pressed her hands against the top of her head, which reeled from the gruesome sight, and followed them inside as they placed the litter with great care in the center of the room and then withdrew. Sofkhatep departed immediately after them and the place was left to her and him. She rushed over and knelt by his side, interlocking her fingers and clasping them tightly in a state of hopeless distress. She looked into his grave and slowly dimming eyes, and as she gasped for breath, her shifting glance was drawn toward his stricken chest. She saw the patches of blood and the arrow protruding and she shivered with unspeakable anguish, as she cried out, her voice disjointed with torment and dread, "They have wounded you. Oh, the horror!"

He lay there, drifting in and out of consciousness, languid and inanimate. The short journey had drained the last dregs of the strength that was already quickly fading. But when he heard her voice and saw her beloved face, a faint breath of life stirred in him and the shadow of a distant smile passed across his clouded eyes.

She had only ever seen him impassioned and bursting

with life like a gusty wind and she almost lost her wits as she beheld him now, like one long since withered and grown old. She cast a burning glance at the arrow that had brought all this about and said as she winced with pain, "Why have they left it in your chest? Should I summon the physician?"

He gathered all his dwindling and scattered strength together and said feebly, "It is no use."

Madness flashed in her eyes and she rebuked him, "No use, my darling? How can you say that? Does our life together no longer please you?"

With desperate weakness he stretched out his hand until it brushed against her cold palm, and whispered, "It is the truth, Rhadopis. I have come to die here in your arms in this place, which I love more than any place in the world. You must not lament our fortune, rather grant me some cheer."

"My lord, do you bring me tidings of your own death? What evening hour is this? And I was waiting for it, my darling, with a spirit consumed with yearning, seduced by hope. I hoped you would come bearing me news of victory, and when you came you brought me this arrow. How can I be cheerful?"

He swallowed his saliva with difficulty, as he pleaded with her in a voice that was more like a moan, "Rhadopis, put this pain aside and come nearer to me. I want to look into your lustrous eyes."

He wanted to see the fresh face radiant with happiness and delight to end his life with that enchanting image but she was enduring pains no human could endure. She wished she could scream and wail and rant and give vent to her tortured breast, or to seek solace in raving madness or the roasting fires of hell. How could she be cheerful and composed and gaze upon him with that face which he loved and which comforted him more than any other in this world or the next?

Still looking at her longingly, he said, "Those are not your eyes, Rhadopis."

With grief and sorrow in her voice, she said, "They are my eyes, my lord, but the spring that gives them life and light has dried up."

"Alas, Rhadopis! Would you not forget your pains this hour just for me? I wish to see the face of my darling Rhadopis, and listen to her sweet voice."

His request pierced her heart and she could not bear to deprive him of something he wanted in this black hour. With great cruelty to herself, she smoothed the surface of her face and forced a trembling smile to her lips. Without a sound she touched him tenderly as she had touched him when he lay as her lover and a look of contentment appeared on his pale and withered face and his pale lips parted in a smile.

If she had been left to her emotions, the world would not have been wide enough to contain her insane ranting, but she yielded to his dear desire and fed her eyes on his face, not believing that it would disappear from her view forever after a few short seconds, and that she would never see it again in this world however much she suffered or sighed or shed tears of grief. His image, his life, and his love would all pass away, distant memories of an unfamiliar past. How preposterous for her broken heart to believe that he had once been her present and her future. And all this because a wild arrow had found its mark here in his chest. How could this despicable arrow put an end to her hopes when the whole world had been too narrow to contain them? The woman let out a deep and fervent sigh that stirred up the fragments of her broken heart. The king was giving up the last remnants of life that still hung on in his breast and rattled in his throat. His strength waned and his limbs went limp, his senses died and his eyes dimmed. All that remained of him was his chest, heaving tumultuously, while therein death and life were locked in desperate and doomed combat. Suddenly his face contorted with pain and he opened his mouth as if to scream or cry out for help and he held the hand that she had extended to him, a look of indescribable panic in his eyes. "Rhadopis, raise my head, raise my head," he cried.

She took his head in her trembling hands and was about to sit him up when he emitted a fearful moan and his hand fell limply at his side. Thus ended the battle raging between life and death. She hurriedly laid his head back in its original position and let out an agonizing high-pitched scream, but it was short-lived and her voice cut off abruptly as if her lungs had been torn out, her tongue turned to stone, and her jaws clamped tightly shut. She stared with emotionless eyes into the face that had once been a person, and sat there immobile.

It was her scream that broadcast the painful news and the two men rushed into the room, unnoticed by her, and stood in front of the litter. Tahu cast a dismal glance at the king's face, the wan pallor of death overspreading his own face, and did not utter a word. Sofkhatep too approached the corpse and bowed in deep reverence, his eyes blinded by tears that ran down his cheeks and dripped onto the ground, saying in a shaking voice whose grieving tones tore at the pervading silence, "My master and lord, son of my master and lord, we commit you to the most exalted gods whose will has decreed this day the beginning of your journey to the eternal realm. How gladly I would sacrifice my doting senility for your tender youth, but it is the immutable will of the Lord. So now farewell, my noble lord."

Sofkhatep stretched out his emaciated hand to the coverlet and unhurriedly drew it over the corpse. Then he bowed once again and returned to his place with heavy steps.

Rhadopis remained on her knees, in a state of utter bewilderment, engulfed in her sorrow, her eyes transfixed inconsolably on the corpse. An unnerving stillness like death had penetrated her body and she displayed not a single sign of life. She did not weep, nor did she scream out. The men stood motionlessly behind her, their heads turned to the ground, when one of the slaves who had carried the litter entered and announced, "The queen's handmaiden."

The men turned to the door and saw the handmaiden enter, deep sadness etched upon her face, and they bowed to her in greeting. She returned the greeting with a nod of her head and cast a glance at the covered body then turned her eyes to Sofkhatep, who spoke in a voice filled with grief. "It is all over, venerable lady."

The woman was silent for a moment like one in a daze, then said, "Then the noble corpse must be taken to the royal palace. That is Her Majesty the Queen's wish, Prime Minister."

As the lady-in-waiting headed for the door, she gestured to the slaves. They rushed over to her and she ordered them to lift up the litter. As the slaves moved forward and bent down over its poles to lift it up, Rhadopis, who had not felt a thing going on around her, suddenly realized with horror what was happening, and in a hoarse incredulous voice she demanded, "Where are you taking him?"

She threw herself on the litter. Sofkhatep stepped over to her and said, "The palace wishes to carry out its duty in respect of the sacred corpse."

The woman, in a state of shock, said, “Do not take him from me. Wait. I shall die on his chest.”

The lady-in-waiting was looking down on Rhadopis, and when she heard her words, she said roughly, “The king’s chest was not created to be a final resting place for anyone.”

Sofkhatep bent down over the grieving woman and, gently taking hold of her wrists, slowly raised her to her feet as the slaves carried away the litter. She managed to free her hands from his and turned her head violently around her but there was no sign on her forlorn face that she recognized any of those who were present, and she cried out in a dismembered voice like the rattle of death, “Why are you taking him? This is his palace. This is his room. How can you subject me to such humiliation in front of him? It does not please my lord that anyone should mistreat me, you cruel, cruel people.”

The lady-in-waiting paid no attention to her and marched out into the garden with the slaves following her, carrying the litter. The men left the room in a silent and subdued mood. The woman was on the verge of madness. For a short moment she was frozen to the spot, but then she shot off behind them, only to find a coarse hand grabbing her arm. She tried to extricate herself but her efforts were to no avail.

She swung round furiously and found herself face-to-face with Tahu.

Tahu's End

She stared at him in disbelief, as if she did not know him. She tried to free her arm but he would not allow her to do so. "Let me go," she said viciously.

Slowly he shook his head from right to left as if to say to her, "No, no, no." His face was terrible and frightening, and a look of insanity flashed in his eyes as he muttered, "They are going to a place where it is best you do not follow."

"Let me go. They have taken away my lord."

He glowered at her and in an aggressive tone, as if he were giving a military order, he said, "Do not challenge the wishes of the queen who now rules."

Her anger abated and turned to fear and she ceased to resist. For once, she gave in, and knitting her brow, she shook her head in confusion as if she were trying to muster her scattered and bewildered powers of comprehension. She stared at him with a look of incredulous denial, and said, "Do you not see? They have killed my lord. They have killed the king."

The phrase "they have killed the king" rang ominously in his ears, almost too dire to comprehend, and the turmoil in his breast subsided as he said, "Yes, Rhadopis. They have killed the king. I for one would never have conceived before today that an arrow could end Pharaoh's life."

And she said with idiotic simplicity, "How could you let them take him away from me?"

He erupted into fits of insane terrifying laughter and said, "Do you wish to go after them? How crazy you are Rhadopis. You are blind to the consequences, sadness must have left you in a stupor. Wake up, temptress. She who now sits on the throne of Egypt is a woman you have treated with great disdain. You snatched her husband from between her hands and pitched her from the lofty peak of glory and felicity into the pits of misery and oblivion. She could, in an instant, dispatch those who would drag you before her shackled in irons, then deliver you into the hands of torturers who do not know the meaning of the word mercy. They would shave your head of its silken hair and gouge out your dark eyes. They would cut off your fine nose and amputate your delicate ears and then drive you through the streets on the back of a cart, a mutilated and repulsive spectacle, displaying you to the malicious delight of your detractors. And the town crier would walk before you inviting them at the top of his voice to behold the pernicious whore who lured the king from himself, then lured him from his people."

Tahu was speaking as if to satisfy some burning thirst for revenge, his eyes shining with a fearsome light, but she was not moved by his words, as though something stood between him and her senses. Oddly silent, she stared at some unseen object and then shrugged her shoulders in blatant contempt. Fury and rage flared up in his heart at her coldness and distraction. The anger rushed from his heart into his hand and he gripped her tightly, feeling an uncontrollable desire to aim a massive blow at her face and smash it to pieces and gratify his eyes with its disfigurement, as the blood spurted from its pores and orifices. He spent a long moment scrutinizing her calm inattentive expression, disputing with his demonic desire. Then she raised her eyes to him but no sign or characteristic of life was visible in them. He was disturbed and his ardor flagged, and a look of startled fright appeared on his face, like one caught red-handed in a crime. His fingers loosened their grip, and he let out a deep heavy sigh, as he said, "I see that nothing concerns you anymore."

She paid no attention to what he said, but then out of the blue she said, as if speaking to herself, "We should have followed them."

"No, we should not," said Tahu angrily. "Neither of us is any use to the world. No one will miss us after today."

Naïvely, calmly, she repeated, "She has taken him from me, she has taken him from me."

He knew that she meant the queen. And he shrugged his shoulders saying, "You possessed him while he was alive. She has taken him back dead."

She looked at him oddly and said, "You fool, you ignorant fool. Do you not know? The treacherous woman killed him so she could have him back."

"Which treacherous woman is that?"

"The queen. She is the one who divulged our secret and stirred up the people. She is the one who killed my lord."

He was listening to her silently, a mocking demonic smile about his mouth, and when she finished speaking he laughed his mad frightening laugh, then said, "You are mistaken, Rhadopis. The queen is neither traitor nor murderer."

He gazed into her face as he took a step nearer to her, and she looked at him, consternation and bewilderment in her eyes, as he said in a terrible voice, "If it concerns you to know the traitor, here he is, standing before you. I am the traitor, Rhadopis, I."

His words did not affect her as he had imagined. They did

not even rouse her from her stupor, but she shook her head lightly from side to side as if she wished to shake off the lethargy and indifference. He was consumed with anger and he grabbed her by the shoulders roughly and shook her violently as he yelled at her, "Wake up. Can you not hear what I am saying to you? I am the traitor. Tahu, the traitor. I am the cause of all these calamities."

Her body shook violently, and she thrashed about wildly and freed herself from his hands. She took a few steps backward as she looked at his startled face with fear and madness in her eyes. His anger and irritation abated, and he felt his body and head go limp. His eyes darkened and he said softly, in sad tones, "I utter these appalling words so candidly because I sincerely feel that I am not of this world. All ties that bind me to it have been severed. There is no doubt that my confession has caused you great consternation, but it is the truth, Rhadopis. My heart was shattered by hideous cruelty, my soul torn apart with unspeakable pains that demented night I lost you forever."

The commander paused to let his troubled breast calm down, and then continued, "But I harbored a hope, and resorted to patience and resignation, and determined sincerely to carry out my duty to the end. Then came that day you called me to your palace in order to reassure yourself of my loyalty. I lost my mind on that day. My blood was ablaze and I became strangely delirious. My madness drove me into the arms of the lurking enemy, and I divulged to him our secret. Thus did the trusty commander turn into the vile traitor, stabbing his comrades in the back."

He was swamped with emotion at the memory, and his face grimaced in pain and grief. He looked cruelly into her panic-stricken eyes as his fury and anger returned, and cried out, "You pernicious and destructive woman! Your beauty has been a curse upon all who have ever set eyes upon you. It has tortured innocent hearts and brought ruin to a vibrant palace. It has shaken an ancient and respected throne, stirred up a peaceful people, and polluted a noble heart. It is indeed an evil and a curse."

Tahu fell silent, though the rage still boiled in his veins, and seeing the torment and fear she was in, he felt relief and pleasure, and he mumbled, "Taste agony and humiliation and behold death. Neither of us should live. I died a long time ago. There is nothing left of Tahu save his glorious, emblazoned uniforms. As for the Tahu who took part in the conquest of Nubia, and whose courage on the field of battle earned the praise of Pepi II, Tahu, commander of the guard of Merenra II, his bosom friend and counselor, he does not exist."

The man cast a quick glance about the room and unbearable anguish showed in his face. He could no longer stand the stifling silence nor the sight of Rhadopis who was transformed into an unfeeling statue. He snorted into the air with bitterness and disgust as he said, "Everything should end, but I will not deny myself the harshest punishment. I shall go to the palace and summon all those who think well of me. I will announce my crime for them all to hear, and I will unmask the traitor who, though his lord's right-hand man, betrayed him in the end. I shall tear off the decorations that adorn my wicked breast, I shall throw aside my sword and plunge this dagger into my heart. Farewell, Rhadopis, and farewell to life that demands from us so much more than it deserves."

With these words Tahu departed.

The End

No sooner had Tahu left the palace than the skiff bearing Benamun Ben Besar docked at the garden stairway. The young man was exhausted, all color drained from his face, his clothes smeared with dust. The unrest he had seen in the city, the raging fury of the people in revolt, had left his nerves in shreds. Only with great effort had he managed to reach his lodgings. The scenes he had encountered on the way there paled in significance next to the horrors that greeted him on the return journey. So it was that he breathed a great sigh of relief when he found himself walking down the garden paths of the white palace of Biga, the summer room lying in front of him a little way ahead. He reached the room, and believing it to be empty, crossed the threshold. He soon realized his mistake, however, when he saw Rhadopis slumped on the divan underneath her magnificent portrait with Shayth sitting cross-legged at her feet, the two of them contained in an unearthly silence. He hesitated a moment. Shayth sensed his presence and Rhadopis turned toward him. The slave stood up, bowed to him in greeting and left the room. The young man stepped over to the woman, beaming with joy, but when he saw the expression on her face all his emotions stood still and he was overcome with anxiety, struck speechless. There was no doubt in his mind that the news of events outside had reached the ears of his goddess, and that the reports of the pains afflicting the people had reflected themselves on her lovely face and clothed it in this coarse mantle of despair. He knelt down in front of her, then leaned over the hem of her dress and kissed it passionately. He looked at her with his two clear eyes, full of compassion, as if to say to her, "I would gladly take upon myself your suffering." The relief that appeared on her face when she saw him did not escape him. His heart raced with delight and his face turned bright red. In a feeble voice Rhadopis said to him, "You took a long time, Benamun."

The youth said, "I made my way through a crashing sea of seething humanity. Abu today has flared up and boiled over, casting burning embers all about, and filling the air with ash."

Then the young man thrust his hand into his pocket, pulled out a small phial, and handed it to her. She took it in her hand and held it tight. She felt its coldness course through her veins and settle in her heart, as she heard him say, "It looks to me as if your spirit carries more than it can bear."

"Sorrows are contagious," she said.

"Then be gentle with yourself. You should not surrender completely to sorrow. Why do you not leave for Ambus for a period of time, my lady, until some measure of calm returns to this place?"

She listened to him, feigning interest, with an odd expression in her eyes, as if she were looking for the last time at the last person she would ever set eyes upon in this world. The thought of death had so completely taken her over that she felt like a stranger in the world. So choked was she by her emotions that she did not feel a drop of compassion for the youth kneeling before her, floating in his world of hopes, his eyes blind to the fate that awaited him so imminently. Benamun thought that she was weighing his proposal in her mind, and hope welled in his heart and his desires were aroused as he said excitedly, "Ambus, my lady, is a town of tranquility and beauty. All the eye sees there is cloudless sky and birds chirping and ducks gliding across the water and lush greenery. Its glorious and happy air will wash away the pains that poor, troubled Abu has roused in your heart."

She soon grew weary of his talking and, as her thoughts wandered to the mysterious phial, she felt a yearning for the end. Her eyes scoured the spot where the litter had lain just a short while before. Her heart screamed out that she should end her life here and now. She decided to get rid of Benamun so she said, "What you are suggesting is wonderful, Benamun. Let me think for a while, alone."

His face shining with joy and hope, the young man asked her, "Will I have to wait long?"

And she said, "You will not have to wait long, Benamun."

He kissed her hand, rose to his feet, and left the room.

Shayth came in almost immediately after, just as Rhadopis was about to get up off her seat, but before the slave could say a word, Rhadopis ordered her away again. "Fetch me a jug of beer," she said, and was rid of her.

Shayth went back to the palace. Meanwhile, Benamun had strolled down to the pool and was resting on a seat by its edge. He was now in a state of rapture and delight, for hope was bringing nearer his goal of taking his beloved goddess to Ambus, far from the misfortune hanging over Abu. Then she would belong to him and he would find comfort with her. He prayed to the gods to come down to her in her loneliness and to inspire her toward the right decision and a felicitous outcome.

He could not bear to sit for long, and he stood up to walk leisurely round the pool. When he had completed the first lap he saw Shayth carrying a jug, making hurriedly for the room. His eyes followed her until she disappeared behind the door. He decided to sit down again and had only just done so when he heard a chilling scream ring out from inside the room. He leapt to his feet, his heart in his mouth, and raced over to the source of the commotion. He found Rhadopis sprawled on the floor in the center of the room, the slave girl kneeling by her side, bending over her, calling her, touching her cheeks, and checking her pulse. He rushed over to her, his legs trembling, panic and alarm clearly visible in his wide eyes. He knelt down next to Shayth and taking Rhadopis's hand between his own, he found it cold. She seemed like one asleep, save that her face was all pale, tinged with a gentle blueness. Her ghostly lips were slightly parted, and locks of her black hair lay disheveled on her breast and shoulders while others had tumbled onto the carpet. He felt his throat slowly parch, his breath unable to escape as he asked the slave in a hoarse voice, "What is wrong with her, Shayth? Why isn't she answering?"

The woman answered in a voice like a wail, "I do not know, sir.

"I found her when I entered the room just as you see her now. I called her but she did not respond. I ran over to her and shook her but she did not come to, and no sign of consciousness showed in her. O Lord, my lady. What is the matter with you? What has afflicted you to make you like this?"

Benamun did not utter a word, but looked long at the woman crumpled on the floor in terrible stillness. As his eyes looked about her they alighted on the fiendish phial beneath her right elbow, the stopper removed. He let out a sorrowful moan as his trembling fingers picked it up. All that remained inside were a few drops clinging to the glass and as his eyes moved between the phial and the woman, the truth became clear. A shudder ran through his slender body that tore him all to shreds. He moaned in agony and the slave turned to him as he exclaimed in a panic-stricken voice, "O God, how terrible!"

Shayth fixed her eyes on him as she asked him in apprehension and alarm, "What is it that horrifies and disturbs you? Speak, man. I am almost out of my mind with confusion."

He paid no attention to her, and addressing Rhadopis as if she could hear him and see him, he said, "Why have you taken your own life, why have you taken your own life, my lady?"

Shayth screamed and beat her breast with her hands, saying, "What are you saying? How do you know she has taken her own life?"

He threw the phial violently against the wall and it smashed into pieces, then he said in bewilderment and dismay, "Why did you annihilate yourself with this poison? Did you not promise me that you would seriously consider coming with me to Ambus, far away from the troubled South? Were you deceiving me so that you could put an end to your life?"

The slave looked at the shards of broken glass, all that remained of the phial, and said in disbelief, "Where did my lady obtain the poison?"

Shrugging his shoulders inconsolably, he said, "I brought it to her myself."

She was filled with rage and screamed at him, "How could you do that, you wretch?"

"I did not realize that she wanted it so that she could kill herself with it. She deceived me, as she did just now."

She turned away from him in dismay and burst into tears, and pored over the feet of her mistress, kissing them and washing them with her tears. The young man was swamped with desolation as he fixed his bulging eyes on Rhadopis's face, which was now shrouded in eternal stillness. He wondered in his desolation how oblivion could apprehend such beauty as the sun never before had shone upon, and how such burning overflowing vitality could quiesce and don this pale and withered hide that would soon display signs of corruption. He longed to see her, if only for a fleeting moment, the breath of life restored to her, her graceful walk, a smile of joy beaming from her resplendent face, an expression of love and seduction. Then he could die and it would be his last memory of this world.

Shayth's wailing irritated him intensely and he chided her, "Cease your racket!"

He gestured to his heart and continued, "Here is the place of noble grief. More noble than weeping and wailing."

There still remained in the slave's heart the faintest glimmer of hope, and looking at the youth through her tears she implored him, "Is there no hope, sir? Perhaps it is just a severe faint."

But in his grief-stricken voice he said, "Neither hope nor expectation shall bring her back. Rhadopis is dead. Love is dead. All my delusions are scattered asunder. Oh, how dreams and delusions toyed with me. Now, though, everything is over. Fearsome death has roused me from my slumber."

The last rays of the sun slipped below the horizon, its blood-red face slowly disappearing in a glowing haze. Darkness crawled in, covering the universe in a raiment of mourning. In her grief, Shayth had not forgotten her duty toward the corpse of her mistress. She was well aware that she would not be able to accord it the reverence and care it was due in Biga while all around her lady's enemies lurked, waiting to sate their revenge upon the body. She confided her fears in the young man whose heart was on fire right next to her. She asked him if the two of them might transport the body to the town of Ambus, and there deliver it into the hands of the embalmers and lay it to rest in the Besar family mausoleum. Benamun agreed with her suggestion, not only in his words but also in his heart. Shayth summoned some slave girls, and they brought in a litter. They placed the body on it and drew a sheet over it. The slaves carried the litter down to the green boat, which immediately set sail down river to the North.

The young man sat at the head of the body not far from Shayth, while a deep silence lay over the cabin. That sad night, as the boat was drawn slowly northwards by the choppy waters, Benamun strayed through distant vales of dreams: his life passed before his eyes, in images following fast upon the heels of one another, depicting his hopes and dreams, the pain and longing he had endured, and the happiness, felicitation, and joy that he had thought would one day be his lot in life. He sighed from the depths of his broken heart, his eyes fixed on the shrouded body upon which his hopes and dreams had been wrecked, scattered asunder, and dispersed, like sweet dreams put to flight when one awakes.